Mrs. Schuyler Crowninshield

Where the Trade-Wind Blows

West Indian Tales

Mrs. Schuyler Crowninshield

Where the Trade-Wind Blows
West Indian Tales

ISBN/EAN: 9783337078959

Printed in Europe, USA, Canada, Australia, Japan

Cover: Foto ©Andreas Hilbeck / pixelio.de

More available books at **www.hansebooks.com**

WHERE THE TRADE-WIND BLOWS

WHERE THE TRADE-WIND BLOWS

WEST INDIAN TALES

BY

MRS. SCHUYLER CROWNINSHIELD

New York

THE MACMILLAN COMPANY

LONDON: MACMILLAN & CO., Ltd.

1898

CONTENTS

v

CANDACE

CANDACE[1]

CANDACE was coming up the hill with the washing. Under Candace, beneath the aparejo upon which she sat, was the back of Winfield Robinson's big black bull. On Candace's head was a basket which contained some of the clean clothes. On one side of the bull hung a small hair trunk in which were corded the Señor's shirts; on the other side was a saddle-bag with bumping sides. Little Malcolm sat in front of his mother, much as he would sit upon the earthen floor of her cabin. He sat sidewise, his bare toes not overlapping the edge of the saddle, it was so broad.

Generally Candace rode the bull without a leader, but as her load was unusually heavy, she had brought her eldest son, Sambo, to act as bull-driver. A bull-driver may lead the bull or may drive him from his seat upon the aparejo. Sambo walked about five feet ahead of the bull, leading him by a rope; the rope was fastened to a ring in the bull's nose. From the nostrils of the animal waved long strings of saliva; his

[1] Căn'dace.

body was wet; his sturdy legs were splashed with the mud of the valley through which he had passed.

They made a picture as they came slowly up the rough, uneven path between the rows of banana trees, now flecked with shadows, and again emerging into the hot white glare. The old fringed leaves of the bananas arched over their heads, and met in places across the path; their shade was grateful. Little Malcolm clasped Candace's dress with one hand; the other was laid confidingly upon the bull's rough neck, slipping back and forth in the shaggy hair as the great head swayed from side to side.

Having reached the kitchen door, this modern though shadowy Europa slid off the aparejo to the veranda steps.

"Pretty hard tug comin' up dese hills," she said pleasantly, showing her white, even teeth as she spoke.

Candace's stiffly starched old dress kept the form of the saddle and went in at the knees behind. It was a faded green muslin. Round her slim throat she wore a red silk handkerchief. She endeavored to smooth down the board-like lace, which had once been the glory of the yoke, but which her unaccomplished laundering had worn into holes. She lifted little Malcolm down; he stood where she placed him — a diminu-

tive fellow, gazing slyly at his bare toes; his fair
curly head and general appearance making him
seem the prototype of the Christ Child in the
picture called the "Holbein Madonna."

Candace had them of all ages and of all
shades. As the shades grew lighter, the names
became more ambitious. Sambo was black as a
coal and just eleven. He could faintly remember his father, who was always called "Nor-
wood's Sam." Polly was tan color; Maria was
what we distinguish as brunette at the North,
when speaking of the child of white parents;
Alicia was Polly's color, with auburn hair; Gladys
was almost fair, with dark eyes and golden hair;
and little Malcolm had a white skin, with light
gray eyes and a curly tow head. As Candace
had lapsed in virtue, she had risen in the social
scale; the terms are synonymous in Haldez.

Winfield Robinson was a fair-haired Scotch-
man, who lived across the hills "Up Haldez
way," on the road to the city. He owned a
great cocoa plantation, and sold his seed to a
large firm in Paris. Candace had charge of his
house and washed for the Colonias [1] near, thus
making a little money for herself. Winton was
standing on the veranda as Candace alighted.
She removed the basket from her head.

[1] *Colonias:* used by the native, indiscriminately, to designate the planter, or the plantation which he owns.

"Dere, Señor Don Carlos, I tol' you I bring some cacao pods," (Candace properly said cacow), "an' I done brung 'em." Candace spoke as had her father and mother over at Saltona. They were two of that colony who had come many years ago from the slave states of North America, and had settled at one or two spots on the shores of the great bay. These people speak the old familiar jargon of the African slave, and this, more than any other circumstance, makes the stranger feel "at home."

In the language of the Island there is no consistency. The tongues vary as they did in the days of the captivity. One hears pure English, pure Spanish, and pure French, occasionally pure German; and one hears each language broken, cracked, or mutilated. Beside these is heard the African patois, mixed slightly or thoroughly, as the case may be, with the broken, cracked, mutilated, or common sort of the tongues of many nations. Added to this, people come from the islands of St. Thomas and Porto Rico, as well as from Turk's Island, to obtain employment on the great banana walks or sugar estates; and they speak the English tongue with pronunciation and intonation as varied and contrasting as are those of our own Maine farmer and the native Virginian.

Sambo tethered the bull to the ring at the corner of the kitchen, then he loosened the small hair trunk from the saddle and set it upon the veranda; next he lifted little Malcolm up out of the mud which was squeezing between his toes, and set him also upon the veranda; then he dislodged the saddle-bag and gave it to Candace. She came up the steps and laid the bag at Winton's feet.

"I done brung de lady some mango, an' some guava seeds. Sam, where dat u'ur sa'l-bag?" Candace opened the bag which she held, and disclosed five or six long green and yellow fruits, with high, rough ridges and deep seams, looking not unlike elongated melons.

"Dose de bes' de Señor Don Win have; he sen' 'em wif his complimen's."

Candace's voice was sweet and low, but it reached a pair of listening ears in the sitting-room. A blond, determined-looking woman came out of a far door which opened upon the veranda; her eye fell upon a tall, straight octoroon leaning against the corner-post. Candace looked up respectfully from under her curling lashes. Madam Winton had her lorgnon in her hand; she raised it to her eyes; they were very searching eyes.

"Whose child is that?" she asked, looking past the cocoa pods.

"He mine, Señora." What pride in Candace's tone!

"Why! he's white!"

Winton looked up quickly. "Mother!"

Candace seemed fairly bursting with importance. She smiled at Madam Winton in a pleased way, showing her pretty white teeth.

"Yes'm," she said.

"*You abandoned woman!*"

"I — I — What, Señora?" as if failing to understand, which indeed she had.

"Mother!" Winton's tone was beseeching.

"I said, *You abandoned woman!*" Madam Winton fixed her gaze on the pretty, shy boy. He looked upward, and catching sight of the long gold chain which held the lorgnon, he made a step forward and held out his hand. Madam Winton drew back.

"Faugh! I wouldn't touch that child with gloves on," she said, and turning, went into the sitting-room.

"I's so'ry," said Candace, whose eyes had filled with tears; she looked from Madam Winton's vanishing skirts to the Señor's troubled face. "I brung de lady some mangos and guava seeds, but," with her head drooping on one side like a chidden child, "I s'pose she won' take 'em now."

"Leave them there on the table, Candace, thank you very kindly; you must not mind my

mother; she has been very nervous; we had a
terrible trip across the bay; perhaps you have
heard : the Señora is quite upset," and then to
change the subject, " How much for the washing, Candace ? "

" De Señor Don Carlos pay me by de mont' ;
hab he forget ? " Candace shook her head,
sighing sadly. " I's so'ry — ve'y, ve'y so'ry."
As if, had she known Madam Winton's preju-
dices in time, she might have remedied the evil.

" Is Malcolm hungry ? Would you like something to eat ? Juan, have you any — "

" No, Señor, I could not eat." Candace stood
erect and dignified ; she moistened her dry lips
between her sentences. " Malcolm must not eat.
No ! no ! wait till Mammy git you home." She
took from the child's clenched hand a square of
cake which Juan had just brought from the
kitchen ; she bent the pink palm outward, picked
from it every crumb, and threw them to the
clamorous chickens. The child wept and gazed
after the dainty ; she soothed him, pressing her
lips to the top of the curly blond head.

" Come, Sambo ! "

Sambo, who had been talking fighting-cock
with Alphonse up behind the kitchen, came
tumbling down the hill. He unfastened the
rope and turned the bull round. The atmosphere was full of sadness. He turned his head

and regarded Winton with a serious, troubled gaze. He helped his mother to the aparejo, and lifted up the child.

"Buen' dia', Señor," said Candace, sadly.

She did not look back, and they vanished down the path over which they had come, the bull's great body plunging from side to side; the banana fringes closing in upon them all, shutting out from sight Candace's pale green gown and red kerchief, and the boy's curly head upon his mother's shoulder.

As they sank below the crest of the hill, Madam Winton came out of the sitting-room. If, you had known Madam Winton, you would have been sure that her first words would be, "Well, I never!" And so they were.

"Has that abandoned creature gone?" A moment of silence, and then the word *"Pollution!"*

"Mother, it was all a mistake your coming here; I see it more plainly every day. But while you do stay, you will have to get used to strange sights. See these curious cacao pods, mother; you open them in this way."

Winton took up his machete and slashed sharply across the fruit. The cut disclosed a milky lining. Winton took from the inside forty or fifty flat brown seeds, and threw them into a pail. In this pail was about a quart of wood ashes slightly moistened. He stirred the seeds gently through the mixture. Madam Winton looked on with unwilling curiosity. When angry with one person she was at loggerheads with the whole world.

"That is to keep the ants away, mother; Pedro and I will plant these pretty soon in the centre of the banana star."

"Banana star?"

Delighted that she showed even a slight interest, he explained. "Four banana suckers planted each at a corner of an imaginary square make the star. Here, let me place these four tumblers at the four corners of my square. Imagine that they are banana plants, or mats, and that each corner is twelve feet away from the next corner. Now, here we have our star; in the centre, just here, we plant our cacao seed. That is called starring."

"Who is the father of that child?"

Winton pushed the tumblers aside; he arose with a sigh and entered the house. He returned in a moment with his broad hat and called, "Get your machete, Pedro; we can finish planting the home field before breakfast."

Winton mounted the hill behind the house with easy strides. He wore a panama hat and a loose striped cotton shirt; round his waist was a tan-colored belt with a pistol-holder; this was empty.   In his hand he carried a machete with which, as he went, he slashed and cut at the ever-encroaching branches and vines.   A small green snake ran across his path ; he stooped and picked it up by the tail, but, responsive to its pleading wriggle, he let it go again.   A deep cut with his machete at a tall young tree; it fell as if it had leaped voluntarily from its trunk, stood up-right for a moment upon its wet white stem, and then toppled over among the dead leaves which had strewn the forest for generations. Winton walked to the branching end of the young tree, and cut deeply into the thick green growth beneath the top of fan-like leaves.

"A cabbage palm, Pedro."   He touched it with the machete only, as the thorns upon its sides looked threatening.   He picked out a bit of the luscious centre and conveyed it to his mouth upon the point of his ever-useful weapon; for the machete is in use every hour of the day among its employers.   It cuts down trees, severs branches and vines, cuts off heads, from the larger animals down to those of the feathered tribe, splits the kindling for the kitchen stove, slays enemies in legitimate warfare, or in a quarrel over a pack of cards, peels potatoes, helps in the building of such houses as the native is competent to make for himself, and finally, in the hand of some one else, digs its owner's grave.

"As sweet as a chestnut from the old woods at home," said Winton. "Don't forget it as we come back."

Winton handed the delicacy to his mother as he came up the veranda steps at eleven o'clock, hot and weary with his morning's work. It was necessary for Winton to make these peace offerings occasionally, because of the morals of the country. It seemed a little hard to him sometimes, as he was not to blame for the lax state of things, and had had no share in promoting it.

As Alphonse was removing the coffee from the breakfast table, he turned.

"If the Don Carlos allow, I should like to attend the fandango at Haldez to-night."

"Very well, Alphonse."

"The domestics of La Floresta will attend in a great mass."

"Very well, Alphonse; go on; that's enough." Evidently Winton was fearful of revelations.

"What is a fandango, Charles?"

"A sort of merry-making, mother." Winton did not add that in the vocabulary of "Las Palmas" the word *fandango* covered a multitude of delights such as cock-fights, gambling, a possible stabbing affray, a possible death. But what would you have? There must be some pleasures in the life of a hard-working peon.

"Who lives at La Floresta?"

"Winfield Robinson."

"Does that woman who was here to-day live with him?"

"She is his housekeeper."

"Oh!" A long silence, broken only by the sound of weeds being torn away from the ground where old Aroya was cleaning round the banana mats.

"Charles, the day that that man Robinson sets foot in this house, that day I leave for home."

"He will have to arrange his dates, then, to accommodate you, mother; the steamers sail only once in two weeks, sometimes at longer intervals."

"Well, well; don't be funny at my expense, Charles; you are often funny without being humorous; all that I say is, when he comes, I go."

Winton puffed his cigarette and sighed and thought. It had indeed been a foolish experiment.

"I might have known it," mused he. "Dear mother has always been of such an inquiring turn of mind. The words *sub rosa* do not exist in her vocabulary."

At one o'clock that night there was a tapping at Winton's door. He thought that he heard a

groan. He pushed open the heavy wooden shutter near his bed.

"Get up, Señor Don Carlos, fo' de lub o'
Gawd, get up!" It was a low feminine whisper.
Winton slipped quietly out into the moonlight.
No toilet was necessary, the costume for day
and night in that country being much the
same.

"You! Candace!" he whispered. Upon the
veranda floor behind her he saw a recumbent
form. Winton lighted a lamp.

"Robinson! How came he here?"

"Oh! Señor, fo' de lub o' Gawd, save him!
He done tuck sick after dey all went off to de
garito,[1]" and then she whispered, "Do you t'ink
any one give him anyt'ing, Don Carlos?"

Winton wondered with her. Robinson's meth-
ods were not always of the most pacific. Tears
were streaming down Candace's face.

"What is it, Charles?"

Madam Winton stood silhouetted in the doorway.

"Mother, there is a man here very ill."

She came quickly toward him. She caught
sight of Candace.

"Oh! it's you," she said.

"Oh! don' min' me, misses; save him, fo' de
lub o' Gawd!"

---

[1] Cock-fight.

"Woman, take not that name upon your lips! Stand aside, Charles." Madam Winton kneeled down by the prostrate form. She placed her finger upon the man's pulse.

"How did you get him here, Candace?"

"On my back, Señor." Winton looked incredulous. Candace insisted in a soft, anxious voice, her eyes fixed all the time upon Madam Winton and the subject of her ministrations.

"Oh! yaas, Señor, I mighty strong. I use' lif' a bar'l flour befo' Sambo done get bawn."

"On your back, Candace, all that long way?"

"Dey tuk de bull to de garito, Señor, and de hosses, dey wanderin'."

"Why didn't you come for me?"

"De Señora she got medicine chis'; I wou'n't ask for *me*, Señor; I poor trash, not wort' savin', but *he!*" and then going quickly to Madam Winton and kneeling beside her, "Oh! Señora, save him fo' de lub o' Gawd."

"Bring me the lamp, Charles. So! hold it there." She rolled back the eyelid, and closely scrutinized the man's eyeball.

"H'm! h'm! Has your master any enemies?"

Candace did not raise her downcast eyes. Madam Winton turned suddenly: —

"You! Black coffee! and quick, do you hear?"

The fire had not gone out in the kitchen stove,

---

[1] Cock-fight.

but before the stimulant had been brought Madam Winton had applied such other restoratives as she knew of.

"Charles! hand me that bottle." Madam Winton gave her orders with the force of a general. One obeyed her instinctively. Winton took a dark blue glass bottle from the chest and began to drop some of the liquid into the tumbler held ready.

"Oh! not that! not that! Look! Charles, couldn't you see?"

Candace stood patiently holding the coffee-tray. She watched the hurried movements of mother and son with bewilderment. Madam Winton took the bottle from her son's hand. She turned it round. Upon its side were a skull and cross-bones.

"Can't you read, Charles? 'External application.' That would have killed him." The symbol of death burned itself in on Candace's brain. She watched Madam Winton as she restored the flask to its place in the chest.

"It would have killed him," said Candace to herself, over and over, "it would have killed him."

Then followed a long night of maltreating with kindest intent the almost unconscious man, in which duty Madam Winton and her son were active workers, and Candace their eager ally,

c

doing with trusting docility what she was ordered.   By morning the man was saved.

"Oh! Señora!"   Candace was kneeling on the floor, clasping Madam Winton's white wrapper between her grateful hands.   "I bless you, I t'ank you; when you want a friend, Candace your friend.   *I* die, make no difference; *he* die!"—a look of utter despair as the gray eyes were rolled upward.

Madam Winton brushed some moisture from her hard, proper, high cheek bone.

"And his wife comes down by this steamer," groaned Winton, when they were alone.

A CHRISTMAS SURPRISE

A CHRISTMAS SURPRISE

It was the day before Christmas. Candace came up the hill again. This time she was walking. She wore a purple calico, old and unstarched, which clung closely to her slight form; her feet were bare, her general air denoted depression and anxiety.

Candace stood for a little while leaning against the pilotillo [1] by the back steps. There was an atmosphere of silence about the house; she scanned the premises with searching eyes, and then, mounting the steps, she went to the door of the sitting-room and tried to open it. The door was securely fastened. Then she turned the handle of the door of the Señor's room: it was locked. Then she went up the hill, and leaned against the side of the kitchen entrance and watched Juan prepare the chocolate for the eleven o'clock breakfast.

"You is inquirin' fo' somet'ing?" asked Juan.

"Want to see de Señor."

"Him an' Pedro gone up de hill — proppin'

[1] From *pilotaje*, the uprights upon which the house is built.

21

bananas; big win' las' night; some blow down. Reckon dose lazy Porto Ricanians git fi'-han'[1] bunches — plenty — plenty."

" Is de Señora at home?"

" She gone up to see de waak; ain' much goin' on she don' know 'bout. Jes' ought to see how caa'ful have to be o' coffee an' beans, now de Señora come."

" She walk?"

" Rode de little black pony. Got a real high-tone' habit f'om de States."

Candace watched Juan in silence as he sprinkled the sugar over the coffee which he was roasting.

" Hab to be mighty caa'ful o' sugar," said Juan, ruefully shaking his head; " not'in' ain' haaf so tasty since de Señora done come." He placed the bowl back upon the little shelf, nailed to the wall, and prepared to mix his biscuits.

" I laike luk at her music."

" Who? De Señora?" Juan shook his head. " She done tuk de key. Hab to wait, Candace, till she come her own se'f."

" Won' you open de do', Juan?" The tone was most persuasive.

" How I ope' de do'? She nebber leab no keys roun'."

Candace turned away and went down the hill. She seated herself on the veranda steps, her eyes

---

[1] Five-hand.

bent dejectedly upon the ground. Sultana, Winton's great hound, came up and nosed about her; Candace pushed the dog away, wearily.

Juan came down to set the table; the sun was growing very hot, and he pushed it more into the shade, where the corner vines sheltered the Señora, at least, thoroughly from the glare. He took a snow-white cloth from the blue chest standing near, laid it smoothly upon the table, and then opened the cupboard and took the necessary plates and cups from the shining row standing there. Candace did not offer to help him, as sometimes she had done; she seemed to have forgotten the world. Juan looked toward her.

"How de chillun, Candace?"

"Well." The tone was utterly listless. Juan looked at her with amazement. Usually Candace was so full of the children, their doings, and sayings. But the breakfast must be ready when the Señora returned, and Juan had no time for speculation.

Candace's thoughts were far distant from "Las Palmas." She broke away, unconsciously, with her slim fingers, part of the shell of the comajens' long covered pathway leading from the pilotillos to the roof, where the little insects had begun to form a nest. When Madam Winton had arrived at the plantation, she had thought

the long brown excrescence a vine which had
grown thus quickly upon the new house. As
the covering fell to the ground and let the light
of day into the passage, the pale brown ants,
looking not unlike animated millet-seed, showed
their distraction by running wildly here and
there, warning their friends in the tunnel of the
strange fate which had befallen them.

"I bu'n dat comahen ncs' to-morrow," said
Juan, as he passed by Candace, carrying the shining silver upon its neat tray.   He had made this
declaration every day for the last two months.
"Dey eat trough a tin ruff, I ve'ly belieb."

Candace made no reply; unconsciously she
continued breaking away the covering until a
long line of wildly scampering insects was ex-
posed. Not until Juan brought the kettle and
deluged the track with a stream of boiling water,
did she desist. When she heard voices from
the hill, Candace arose and stood, respectfully
waiting.

Down they came; Winton leading on a powerful gray, the Señora following upon her small
black, Pedro holding the bridle rein. A large
tree felled by the previous night's wind lay
across the path, and there would lie forever if
left to native energy to remove. The gray
leaped the obstruction with ease, the black
scrambled over aided by Pedro's urging rein.

" Well!   I'm glad to get home alive !   Why !
There is that girl again.   What do you want
now ? "   Madam Winton's tears were not so
near the surface as they had been a few nights
before.

"Come to see Don Carlos got any mo' washin'."

Winton looked at the woman in astonishment.

" Washing ?   Candace, you took it only Mon-
day.   I never give it to you twice a week."
Candace looked abashed.

" I laike luk at de Señora's music, after she
done eat."

" The piano !   I can't be troubled with her,
Charles; besides, she disgusts me !   The sight
of her irritates me."

" I laike to buy one," said Candace, looking
at the Señor.

" My poor girl ! do you know what a piano
costs ?   And you could not play it."

Candace raised her eyes at Winton's kind
tone, and then she unknotted a handkerchief
that she carried, and produced six Mexican
dollars.   She held the silver toward Winton.
He shook his head pityingly, as we do at the
ignorance of a little child.

" The piano cost more than fifty times that
sum, Candace.   Perhaps the Señora will play
for you, sometime."

The Señora's stern face gave no assent.   Candace replaced the silver in her handkerchief and reknotted it.

"Come to breakfast, Charles." Madam Winton had seated herself in the corner of the veranda where the bougainvillea vine made for her a perfect screen. Some green and brown lizards ran down the vine and stretched their pointed heads toward the spotless cloth. Madam Winton drove them away with a fierce "Shoo!" and a quick snap of her napkin. Candace moved a step nearer the table.

"My li'l Gladys, she pow'ful sick."

"What's the matter with her? Why didn't you say so before?" The sympathies of the domestic healer, lying dormant in all mothers, were aroused. "Headache? fever? chills? any eruption? is she wakeful? When did you notice it first? Is it at all like the calentura[1]? Come right in here."

An indescribable gleam of triumph shone through the slits that Candace made of her eyelids.

"Calentura mighty bad dis year," she murmured. She followed Madam Winton into her room; she passed the piano by unheeding. Madam Winton opened the door of the small cabinet which stood upon her table. She took out a vial, and held it up to the light.

[1] Native fever.

"There! It seems to me that this tincture will be just the thing that you need. Stop! Let me get an empty bottle from the Señor's room" Madam Winton's stiff skirts swished through the opening; then she stepped to the back door of her son's room. "Juan," she called, "take this vial and scald it well." When she returned, Candace was standing demurely looking at the piano.

When Candace was out of hearing — "Do you think she'd take anything, Charles?" asked Madam Winton.

"Honesty itself, mother; I have proved her in too many ways to doubt her now. Oh! Candace," he called loudly, "stay and let Juan give you some breakfast," but Candace gravely shook her head. She stopped at the brow of the hill and looked back at them, then turned and walked rapidly down the slope; when she reached the bottom land she ran, the knotted handkerchief swinging heavily in her hand.

"Poor girl!" said Winton, sighing deeply. He was tempting a large brown lizard with a lump of sugar. "Robinson's wife has arrived at Puerto la Mar; the consul at Caño Sandros has had a cable. I suppose she'll come up here to-day or to-morrow. You know her brother Fenno is in the custom house over there." Winton's tone was gloomy.

"You ought to warn her, Charles."

"I'm afraid I'm not entirely prepared to meet my God, mother."

"Charles!" Madam Winton's tone voiced her horror. "Don't be so irreverent!"

Winton turned in his chair and faced his mother.

"I don't intend to be irreverent, mother, certainly not before you; I mean exactly what I say. I have never found it profitable in this country to interfere with other people's business. We may make a moderate fortune by attending strictly to our own affairs; we shall, perhaps, lose our lives as well as our property, if we try to attend to those of other people. See how that bougainvellia vine is growing over the veranda, mother; it is quarrelling already with the allemanda for the sunniest spot."

"I'm sure they are all sunny enough." Madam Winton wiped her face incessantly. "I shall have to change everything, I get so heated in this fearful breeze, it is so dangerous!"

Winton thought the breeze delightful, but wild horses would not have torn that conviction from him by word of mouth. He had learned that there are times when silence is golden; this was one of them. He sat and smoked. He heard his mother opening and shutting bureau drawers, pulling out fresh clothing, etc. She called to him, her voice sounding plainly through the cracks of the partition.

"Wasn't it strange, Charles, that that girl never mentioned the child's being ill when we came home?"

"Yes, it was queer."

"First, she asked for more washing, and on Wednesday too, and then she wanted to buy a piano for six dollars — Mexican dollars! After that she seemed to remember that her child was ill."

"Yes, it was queer," Winton repeated. He sat and smoked and pondered. A strange people this among which he had taken up his abode! How queerly Candace had behaved! What could have been her motive? The banana fringes rustled as the wind blew strongly up from the bay, the soft breeze fanned his brown cheek; he lazily smoked and thought of many things: whether Pedro had found those missing picks which he insisted had been taken from their hiding-place under the house; whether the incoming steamer would bring him the chairs that he had ordered from the North; whether the *colono* next to his place would send up the yagua[1] as he promised by the next fruit train. Promises, alas! are made to be broken in the Island; whether Francisco had found the

[1] Yagua: dried leaves of the palm, used for thatching the roofs.

little bull which had strayed away; and with
all these wonderings, his thoughts always reverted to Candace and her unusual behavior.
Suddenly he bounded from his chair.

"Mother! mother!"

The crackling of starched skirts ceased.

"Quick! mother, let me in."

"How impetuous you are, Charles." Madam
Winton threw a light shawl over her shoulders.
"Can't you wait a moment?"

"No! Not an instant. The key of your cabinet quick, mother." The doors were wrenched
open. "Ah! I feared so! Pedro." He flung
wide the door. "Saddle the gray at once!"

"Charles, are you crazy?"

"Jim done tuk de gray down to de potrero,[1]
Don Carlos."

"Give me the saddle then; or no — I don't
need it, — the bridle; thanks. Look out for the
Señora." And he was gone, tearing down the
path, dripping streams of water under the tropic
sun. The gray had wandered; it took some
time to find him, but catching the animal and
vaulting upon his back were almost simultaneous
movements, and then came a wild race across
rough fields and over cleared land, regardless of
fallen logs, "banana trash," or other impedi-
menta.

[1] Pasture.

At the primitive railway track, which ran through the plantation, Winton's progress was barred by the stoppage of a train. An engine, with a platform car attached, had just drawn up at the crossing, and, as he neared the place, a small, fair woman was stepping down upon a chair held by a man whom Winton recognized as Fenno, of whom he had spoken to his mother but an hour ago. A little child was standing by the track.

"Hullo, Winton!" It was Fenno's voice.

"For God's sake, back that train!" Winton's voice was hoarse, his look wild.

"The men are unloading the yagua for your new stables, Señor. It won't take long."

"Back down, for the love of God, Garcia; you won't be sorry." Winton's wild appearance argued for immediate action; added to this, he was popular among the peons. Garcia ordered the men to cease unloading; then the signal was given, and the train rumbled slowly backward over the weed-choked ties, leaving the crossing free.

"My sister, Mrs. Robinson, Winton. What a surprise for Robinson, eh?"

A man of less deep feeling would have seen a grim humor in the situation. Winton mechanically touched his hat, hurrying across the grass-grown track. The little girl in Mrs. Robinson's arms gazed wonderingly at the unceremonious stranger.

"Pardon me," he said; "I am in great haste."

Fenno's horses had been taken from the train, and were standing with their black and ragged grooms on the further side of the track.

Winton did not wait to see Mrs. Robinson's descent from the rough ties to the path below. He drove his spurs into the gray; but the animal had been hard worked that morning, and was not of his master's mind. Winton endeavored to spur him on. A little spurt, and then a slow jog-trot. Winton groaned despairingly. The voices of Fenno and his sister could be heard a little distance behind. Would the long winding way never end? Fenno's horses were fresh; he would arrive as soon as Winton. How endless the rough, uneven road, how jaded and tired the gray! At last! at last! there shone the white fence in the distance. He urged on the weary horse with spur and whip. Round on the further side was Robinson's gate. The brother and sister had gained upon him. They were close behind; so close that he could hear their words.

"Win live in such a place? I could not have believed it." The sweet voice was full of astonishment. Fenno said something about her having to get accustomed to a new country, and the three horses entered the enclosure together, the grooms splashing and clattering after. Candace stood in the doorway, shading her eyes with her hand.

" Where is the Señor, Candace?" Winton's excited shout brought a look of surprise to the faces of the others.

" He inside," answered Candace, shortly.

" Don't, man; we want to surprise him." Fenno's tone was reproachful.

" Papa's Christmas surprise," said the young mother, pressing her cheek against the child's.

" Why doesn't he come out?" Winton asked the question authoritatively, ignoring Fenno's gesture to keep silent.

" Can't," said Candace, and spoke truly.

" Lift the little lady down," said Fenno, condescendingly, to Candace; " she is the Señor Don Win's little girl."

Candace looked at the child, and then at Malcolm, who was sitting on the veranda steps. She took the child in her arms, and set her down not ungently by Malcolm. Gladys stood looking shyly on. Winton had vanished inside the house. He came out hurriedly; his face had lost its color.

" Don't go in, Fenno," he said in an undertone; " keep your sister away." But she was on the ground, and mounting the rickety steps.

D

" Why ? is he asleep ?   That does not matter;
we will awaken papa, won't we, little Molly ?"
The child had her arm round Malcolm's neck,
and was kissing her new-found playfellow.   The
young woman took the child's hand, raised her,
and pushed past Winton.

" I beg of you," he urged.   His agitated tone
did not deter her ; she was at the door of the
room, and now she had entered, and had fallen
upon the bed.

" Win, my husband, waken ! speak to me !   Are
you ill, Win ?   I have come so far to see you ;
and here is Molly, little Molly."   She lifted the
child across her husband's body, and seated
her between him and the wall.   The child laid
her hand upon her father's fair curls.   Winton
was crowding a blue glass vial into his pocket.
Candace, dishevelled and unkempt, stood leaning
against the doorpost, gazing stolidly at the pale
young woman who knelt by the bedside.   Her
hat had fallen off, her heavy hair had fallen
down ; she was kissing the cold face, the eyes,
the mouth, in the abandonment of grief.   Candace's eyes were dry.

PAUL DEMARISI'S MORTGAGE

PAUL DEMARISI'S MORTGAGE

INEZ was washing down by the river. She stood upon a broad, flat stone which seemed the end of all things. The river was turbulent and swollen; this argued that there had been heavy rains in the mountains. The water was rising fast. When Inez first came down to the washing-place it had been a foot below where she stood; now it was lapping about her feet. It was warmer than the stone upon which she stood, and felt grateful to her. The river had come rushing along, through sunny fire-swept lands where all the trees had been burned off to give space for the planting of the banana and cacao, and the hot planet had warmed it as it ran.

At Inez's left, the bank faced her in a solid wall of clay, so that, lean out as far as she could, she could not see any one upon her cwn bank of the river. At her right, the path sloped upward, wide and straight, and parallel with the river. At her back was a steep bank overgrown with mosses, and plants, and vines,

which latter forced their way through the dead
leaves of centuries.   Inez's bull, which was tethered at the top of the path, was browsing quietly;
waiting with patience for such time as Inez
should have finished washing, when she would
place her basket upon the aparejo, mount beside
it, and drive home through the wood.   As Inez
worked, she sang some snatches of La Paloma,
that song which had been imported into her
island home from Mexico, and adopted almost as
a national air.

Across the river, but some distance below
the spot where Inez was standing, Juan Romero
was sawing off branches.   They splashed into
the river, and were borne away by the flood.
The possessions of the great cacao company
reached the bank on that side.   The company
had made the mistake of not clearing their land
in the beginning, and they were now, at great
expense and at a very late day, trying to get rid
of too great an abundance of shade.

After a while the sawing ceased.   Cessation
of sound caused Inez to raise her eyes.   Juan
Romero had his hand held over his brow, and
was gazing across the river to the same side, but
some hundred yards below where Inez was employed.   Then she heard a splashing of hoofs, a
shout, and a moment later Señor Don Paul
came in sight, swimming his big roan across;

for the water had risen so high that the ford
was of no use to him.   Over Don Paul's shoulders ran a stout cord, and to that cord was fastened a bag, — a heavy bag, if one could judge
by the way in which it clung to Don Paul's
slight form.   Inez watched the young man in
his passage across, as did Juan Romero.   The
water whirled and swirled in eddies; the horse
pushed bravely on.   Don Paul laid down with
his head on the horse's neck, his feet upon his
flanks.   The middle of the river was reached,
when the rider shouted and turned, clutching
wildly at the horse's side.   He very nearly lost
his hold.

Inez could not discover at first what was the
matter; then she perceived that the heavy bag
was slipping from the cord which had been
trusted to hold it.   It was swinging low at the
side of the animal, who showed signs of fear,
even as he swam, at so unaccustomed a pressure.
Don Paul sat up, his knees in the water; he
clutched desperately at the cord, — the bag; but
the parcel was of great weight, and, sliding
along the cord, at first slowly, and then with a
rush, it disappeared below the muddy waters.
All this happened in a moment, and Inez on her
side of the river, and Juan Romero on his,
watched, open-mouthed.   There was no stopping
for Don Paul.   His horse could not turn, and if

he could, of what avail? The water might rise many feet higher before it subsided, and no one could surmise when that would be. With a shout of despair, Don Paul threw himself again upon his horse's neck. The animal swam with purposeful energy, and, before many minutes had passed, he and his rider had reached the little sand cove where the ford ended.

Inez looked up at Juan Romero. He had shrunk to his smallest possible size. He was standing upright beside the tree trunk in full view of Inez, so that Don Paul, should he raise his eyes, could not see him. If Don Paul said anything, Inez could not hear it. She saw him turn in his saddle, wave his hands with a gesture of despair toward the yellow river, and then he struck spurs to his horse, and vanished along the forest road.

"Goin' to pay de moggage to-day, so Luis say," said Inez, aloud. "Reckon de moggage done got sink." Inez, like most of the people of her island, had two or more languages at command. She spoke readily the patois of the American negro, or the language of the dignified Spaniard. When she communed with herself, it was sometimes in the negro dialect that had been her northern mother's. When she conversed with gentlemen like Don Paul or Don César, it was either in the language of Spain or its rigid translation.

Don Paul rode hurriedly on toward Puerto la Mar. He knew not where to turn. The money was to have been paid that day to the Alcalde who held the mortgage on La Paciencia, the name of Don Paul's hacienda. This title had typified the feelings of the Alcalde. He had waited for some months, the payments being overdue. And now the money was gone, — that money for which he had worked, thought Don Paul, as no gentlemen ever had worked before or since. He could, it is true, come down and live on the bank of the river, and remain there day and night until the water should fall. Even then he might find that the bag had broken, and many of his precious dollars had been swept away in that wild and boiling flood. The dollars that he had slaved for, working with his gang of men for all the colonias near, getting paid small earnings grudgingly; but, finally, the land was his own, his father's honor was saved, and now — " Caramba! why could I not have waited for a few days? the river rises; if I could not go to pay him, neither could he come to foreclose; but a man and his money are soon parted," thought Don Paul, " though I do differently translate it to myself. We say in sunny Spain : —

> " 'A woman, a dog, and a walnut tree,
> The more you beat them, the better they be.'

Henceforth I shall add to that precious list the idiotic fool who is in such haste to pay money to the Alcalde that he cannot wait until the river is low."

He further mused: "What is the use of my going forward? what shall I gain? If I make my old, time-worn excuses, will the Alcalde listen? Assuredly not! Better return,—swim across again while I can. The Alcalde will hear of the rise of the waters," Don Paul added, with a grim smile, "but not of the fall of silver." Don Paul thought this a very fine joke; and, although it was a joke against himself, he chuckled. For a handsome man, he was rather a stupid one in some ways. Handsome men usually have their wits sharpened earlier in life than ugly ones. They come oftener in contact with those sharpeners of wits,—women.

"There is just one thing on which I can congratulate myself," thought Don Paul. "No one saw me lose my bag, and, therefore, no one knows of the presence of the money in the river. Now, what shall I do? Let me think." Don Paul was about to turn, when he spied a man coming toward him. The man was coming from the direction of Puerto la Mar. It was Tres Pelos. Tres Pelos lived in the cepo, usually, as much as outside of it; but this was because he would steal bananas. No one had ever caught Tres Pelos in a greater theft, and he had grown up at La Paciencia under Don Paul's father, the old Señor Don Paul Demarisi. Tres Pelos was fond of the drink of the country; that was his failing. He was, perhaps, a broken reed; but, then, he was a reed of some sort, which is better than nothing at all. Don Paul turned his horse across the roadway, and waited until Tres Pelos drew near.

Tres Pelos wore an apology for trousers, and his shirt was split and torn in many places, showing his ebony skin beneath. His feet were bare and bound with healing leaves; he limped; his head was tied round with a cloth.

"Buen' dia', Señor Don Paul," said Tres Pelos, as he came toward the young man. His face lighted up at the sight of him as it did for no one else. Not even Dolores could win from Tres Pelos such a smile as he gave to Don Paul, whom he had watched grow like a young and royal palm. For the Demarisi family were royal to Tres Pelos, and, indeed, to many beside, though their fortunes had long since failed.

"Buenos dias, Tre' Pelo'," answered Don Paul. "From the cep'[1] again? Poor fellow! No shoes?"

"I could not wear them, Don Paul, even if I had them," said Tres Pelos, in a voice of hope-

---

[1] *cepo.* Used indiscriminately by the native to designate the prison or the stocks.

less monotony. "My ankles are chafed from the stocks. I go to bathe them in the river." Tres Pelos spoke a mongrel sort of Spanish, to which Don Paul had been accustomed from childhood. The river! At these words, Don Paul's thoughts instantly reverted to the loss from which, for a moment, they had wandered.

"Oh, that river! It has risen, Tre' Pelo'. The ford was bare last night." Don Paul ended with a groan: Had but the ford been bare this morning!

"How high, Señor Don Paul?"

"Up to the trunk of the old mahogany."

"Then I cannot get to Paciencia, Don Paul."

"No, Tre' Pelo'. If my roan could carry double, I would take you behind me; but the flood is growing swifter every moment. I must hasten back."

"Then I must remain on this side, Señor?" asked Tres Pelos, ruefully.

"It is the only thing to do, Tre' Pelo'. Now listen. I must talk fast. Do not speak; let me talk. There is an old casa down the bank, a hundred yards below the ford. You know it well. We always called it 'The Rancho.' You remember the little house that my father built for me there, when, as a boy, I started my small colonia dependent on my father's estate?"

"I helped build it, Señor. I, myself, thatched it with yagua."

" Very well. I want you to go there, Tre'
Pelo', and remain until the water subsides."

" I have no food, Señor."

"Do not talk, Tre' Pelo'; your part is to listen."
Don Paul had turned his horse, and was walking
him back toward the ford. Tres Pelos walked
beside him. " You know that, from the earliest
times, I have owned that strip below the ford; that
I tried all manner of fruit-raising down there.
My land runs some two hundred terreas back into
the wood, and adjoins Brandon's colonia. There
are bananas growing on that land, as you know,
— apple bananas, fig bananas, and some plan-
tains. You may live at The Rancho, Tre' Pelo'.
You may build a fire, you may gather and cook
five-hand bunches, and, when they are gone, you
may begin on the six-hand bunches." Tres
Pelos's eyes grew round at the thought of all
this luxury. " You may gather what mangos
you need, and some guavas ; each day you may
pick up the mamey apples that you find on the
ground ; but you must not climb the trees.'
Don Paul did not say that his reason was that
no one might discover Tres Pelos's presence at
The Rancho. "You may, upon occasions, cut
a small cabbage palm." Tres Pelos's eyes grew
rounder. " You may shoot the parrots that fly
overhead, — a shot may come from anywhere, —
and, if the mountain doves come near the place,

you may kill what you need." Tres Pelos's eyes had not alone reached their utmost stretch; his mouth followed suit. Had he been offered a palace, it would not have meant to him half that Don Paul's offer conveyed. Shelter in the blessed island, freedom from the cep' and the stocks, and plenty of food, was better a thousand times than the traditional castle in Spain.

The two men had now reached the ford. The sand cove had been covered with water during Don Paul's absence. The river was creeping up toward the level where they stood. Then Don Paul began to speak more quickly.

"I must get home, Tre' Pelo'. No, stop! I can trust you; you have always been faithful to the Demarisis, whatever you have been to others. The Rancho stands upon the little hill, as you know; the water cannot reach you." Don Paul felt in his pockets; he drew forth some matches and a bunch of trabucos; these he thrust into Tres Pelos's willing grasp. He laid an impressive hand upon Tres Pelos's shoulder. "Tre' Pelo', I have to-day lost a bag full of money,— silver,— there at the ford. Twelve hundred and fifty good dollars, fresh from the bank at Saltona! They lie there on the bottom. They are my all. Live here, Tre' Pelo'; watch the water, and, when it falls, be it day or night, as soon as you can wade, start across the ford

and save them. If you save them, Tre' Pelo',
you save me; if you lose them, I am lost. I
can trust you, Tre' Pelo'; you have no rum;
that is my safeguard."

"Bieng, Señor," said Tres Pelos, without comment. He started down the bank of the river
toward The Rancho. He did not look back.
Before him loomed a blissful vision of a supper
of boiled bananas, a smoke afterward, and a
sleep upon a bed of freshly piled banana leaves.
Paradise to Tres Pelos, whose home had been
the cep', whose rest the stocks!

As Don Paul started his roan down the bank,
he saw a man coming from the wood above the
ford. It was Juan Romero. He carried an axe
and a saw. In his belt were two machetes;
over his shoulder was slung a long shot gun.
Don Paul stopped for a short moment.

"Where have you been, Juan Romero?" he
shouted. The waters were hissing and rushing
so wildly, that, at first, Juan Romero could not
hear. He put his hand behind his ear, and bent
his head forward. The question was repeated.
Juan Romero pointed up the river.

"Sawing limbs up at Cuba Libre.[1]" Juan
Romero did not waste words for politeness' sake.
As Cuba Libre was situated a mile above where
the men met, Don Paul felt quite easy.

[1] The name of a Plantation.

As Don Paul started down the slope, Juan Romero walked down to the edge of the bank, and, shading his eyes with his hand, looked upward to the place in the great tree where he had been sawing limbs.

"No fresh cuts this side, — too many leaves," he said silently. "He won't look back, anyway." He wheeled about, and his gaze rested upon the tattered back of Tres Pelos, who was rapidly disappearing in the distance along the river bank. Juan Romero started in the same direction. He strode quickly, and soon overtook Tres Pelos. Tres Pelos greeted him surlily; he had no mind to share his empire with Juan Romero.

"Buen' dia'," said Juan Romero.

Tres Pelos gave a short nod. Constant acquaintance with the cep' had removed from him any small amount of veneer which he had possessed in days gone by.

"You go, where?" asked Juan Romero.

"That concerns not you," answered Tres Pelos, as he limped along.

"You go to sleep in the little hill-house."

Tres Pelos walked on without speaking.

"I go to keep you company."

"You do not."

Juan Romero unslung his gun, and looked carefully at the cartridge.

"My gun has not been discharged for some

days. It goes off accidentally sometimes. It is a very good gun."

Tres Pelos looked a trifle uneasy, and a more complacent smile began to steal over his features.

"The dove is needed for the sin coche,[1]" mused Tres Pelos; "the agopete[2] is needed for the dove; besides, it might go off accidentally, and who would know?" Tres Pelos smiled, and spoke what he called English to show his ease.

"Mucha please wiz youah company," he said. Juan Romero looked at Tres Pelos out of the corners of his evil eyes.

"We will take the fig banana; we will make the stew. The Don Paul cannot cross the river for days and days."

"Iah needa not to deceive," said Tres Pelos. "I was educate Christian. Iah read my Eerglisha Bib'e. Ah haf raight to take all, everysing. Ze Señor Don Paul gif me raight."

"Aha!" said Juan Romero to himself, with the keenness of a special detective. They came to a banana mat, upon whose thick, yellowbrown stalk grew a large bunch of green bananas ready for cutting. Juan Romero raised his machete; Tres Pelos caught his hand in mid-air.

"Nin'-han'."[3]

"And what of that?"

---

[1] Native stew. [2] Escopete-gun. [3] Nine-hand.

E

" No nin'-han', — no.   No six-han', — no.
When fi'-han' bunch all gone, — zen, yes."   Juan
Romero had his own reasons for not angering
Tres Pelos seriously.   He lowered his machete.
But soon was heard the sharp juicy slash of this
native weapon, and the creak and final ripping
and cracking sound of the breaking trunk.
With a long swish, the great banana tops fell
crashing upon the dead leaves.   The stalk sac-
rificed, the five-hand bunch was cut from it, and
taken to The Rancho.

" You go to the river for water, Tre' Pelo'.   I
peel the banana."   When Tres Pelos returned
with the water, the bananas had not been peeled.
Juan Romero would not even drag the great
iron pot to the fireplace, nor gather the sticks
and banana " trash " to make a fire.   He took
upon himself the rôle of guest.   Tres Pelos regarded him disapprovingly once or twice ; but
he always forced his features into a semblance
of a smile when Juan Romero looked his way.
Did not Juan Romero have the gun ?   When
the supper, which Tres Pelos had prepared and
cooked, was eaten, Juan Romero drew from his
pocket a flat bottle.

" It is not the pink rum of the vega, Tre'
Pelo', but very good for all that.   Let us drink
to the health of the Señor Don Paul, who allows
us to live in his fine Rancho upon the little hill-

top. Where had the Señor Don Paul been when you saw him, Tre' Pelo' ? "

" Pay ze moggage," answered Tres Pelos, with a cunning twinkle of the eye. Juan Romero caught the twinkle, and his small eyes winked still more cunningly.

" And how much was the mortgage, Tre' Pelo' ? "

" Twe'f hundred fifty; Mex. Alcalde haf 'em now at Puerto la Mar. Señor Don Paul, my Señor Don Paul, a free colonia," asserted this loyal liar.

Juan Romero recalled the shout, and the slipping of the bag. Twelve hundred and fifty Mexican dollars! — that was indeed worth scheming for. He recalled the fact that the Señor Don Paul had returned within a quarter-hour's time. Puerto la Mar was certainly an hour away, even if one rode fast.

Meanwhile Don Paul Demarisi had put spurs to his horse, and had struck out into the stream. The water was flowing rapidly, more rapidly than before, and the roan had a struggle to cross, — a feat which few unaccustomed horses could have accomplished. At last, wet and dripping, the pair arrived upon the further shore, but some distance below the ford. Up the steep hill the weary animal scrambled, and, at length stood, panting and trembling, upon the top. As Don Paul rode along in the deepening twilight which lasts so short a time in that tropic land, he saw, ahead of him, a woman. She was riding upon a bull. Upon each side of her slim figure he saw the protruding edges of a basket. She held the basket in front of her. It was piled high with wet, white linen.

"Have you been to the river, Inez?" asked Don Paul, after the customary "Buenos dias."

"Si, Señor."

"Where were you, Inez, — above or below the ford?"

"I was up far, far above the ford; I was opposite Cuba Libre."

Don Paul sighed with relief.

"Then you saw Juan Romero sawing branches at Cuba Libre?"

"Oh, si, Señor! I saw Juan Romero cutting the branches, certainly." Inez could not resist adding, "But Juan Romero did not see me."

Don Paul drew another long breath of satisfaction. So no one but Tres Pelos knew of his loss. Wild horses could not drag his secret from Tres Pelos. Don Paul had not forgotten that rum might accomplish what wild horses would fail to achieve, but Tres Pelos had no rum, and no money wherewith to buy it. Don Paul did not trust any native overmuch, and he was not ignorant of the fact that he was

riding abreast of as colossal a liar as the island
could produce, always excepting Tres Pelos; but
Tres Pelos lied for a purpose. Inez also might
be said to lie for a purpose, — that of keeping
her hand in. It is a mistake to lose practice in
any art in which one has once become proficient.

"I shall wash at the lower ford hereafter,
Señor."

"You shall? And why? Is not the river
equally muddy everywhere?"

"Si, Señor, but the stone is better and broader
below the ford, and it is nearer my home."
Inez, because she possessed a secret, was desir-
ous of explaining her actions, although no one
suspected her.

"You will be almost opposite my little hill-
house, and the old fruit farm that I planted so
long ago."

"Shall I, Señor? I know the opposite bank
so little. I never cross the ford; Luis always
goes to Puerta la Mar when one has to go."
Inez believed that words were given us to conceal thought and action. She had been at the
Demarisi Rancho only the previous week; for
no special purpose but that of keeping up with
the times and learning if there was anything
going on which she ought to know.

"I have allowed Tres Pelos to live there
for a while. I gave him permission to-day,"

said Don Paul, whose secret burned within
him.

"Now, what was that for?" asked Inez of
herself. Inez did not mention having seen Don
Paul and Tres Pelos in conversation as she left
her washing-place, nor did she say that she
had seen Tres Pelos start suddenly toward The
Rancho as if he had a special errand in that
direction. But she was sharp, was Inez, and she
had a way of putting this and that together.

When the horse of Don Paul, following the
bull of Inez, reached the path which branched
off toward the bodega of Padre Martinez, and
so on to La Paciencia, Don Paul said a pleasant
"Buenos dias," and, spurring on the roan who had
been retarded by the bull, he rode rapidly away.

There is not much to interest one in the wilds
along the river bank, and, at home, if you see
that there are no spiders in the room at nightfall, and that the children have their supper of
beans and rice, and are put to bed before the
faint light fades quite away, you have not much
more to think of until the next day. Unless,
indeed, you are willing that the children should
remain up to play with the cucullas,[1] which will
light them to bed as well as any candle. The
little ones safe in their cots, Inez was left to her

[1] A common beetle of the tropics, which shows two bright
lights from its head, and one from the under side of its body.

own thoughts. The moon had not arisen, and she would not burn a precious candle for herself alone. She was anxious about the river. It was rising steadily, and Luis was away at Caño Sandros. Perhaps he could not get back! The water might flood the valley. Perhaps Inez and the children would not be able to flee in time, should the water come creeping in at the kitchen door as it had in days gone by; when Inez, Luis, children, old Señorita the dog, and all the hens and fighting cocks, — the chickens in a basket, — had been forced to take to the rafters, and sit there one entire night until help came in the shape of Dugaldo's flatboat, which had been punted up to Haldez for a load of pineapples. The boat came bumping against the yagua thatch, at three o'clock in the morning. They had been saved, to the smallest chick, human or feathered. The horror of that night Inez never forgot; but, like the Swiss on the sides of their mountains, she loved her home better than her safety.

When the children finally slept, Inez opened the door of her cabin, and stepped to the edge of the bank. How bright the flood! glittering in the light of the moon, like oily, watered silk. Twigs, branches, banana stalks, cacao limbs, went tearing by. Inez stepped to the corner of the henhouse, and, from a low tree growing near,

she picked an aguacate pear. She descended
the bank as far as she dared, and laid the fruit
upon a flat ledge of stone, an inch or so above
the glancing water. She then returned through
the solitary and wonderful night. How lonely it
was! She was miles from any other habitation if
she excepted that of the hill Rancho, and that was
separated from her cabin by the roaring torrent.

Inez stopped at the corner of the house to
give the bull a sympathizing pat. She had tethered him close by the doorway. The great creature seemed to know that mischief was abroad.
He had not laid himself down, but stood ex-
pectant, his broad back ready for its burden.
A half hour later, the wakeful Inez opened her
door, and descended the bank. The pear lay
where she had left it. The stone was not damp.
Another half hour of watching showed that the
river had not increased. Clearly it was not to
be a great flood. Then Inez untied the bull, and
led him away to his familiar tethering-tree. She
returned to her cabin, and, bolting her door, she
laid herself down by the little Laura, and slept.

When Inez went to the new washing-place on
the following day, the river had fallen, perhaps
an eighth of an inch. She took no linen with
her, for she had none to wash, and the stone of
which she had spoken to Don Paul was sub-
merged; but she climbed up into a giant ceiba

tree, and out upon a limb which reached over the water. From this point, as she had well known for years, she could look through a vista among the trees on the opposite bank, and directly into the small clearing, — the clearing which surrounded the little casa upon the hill-top. As Inez watched, a man came out of the house. It was Juan Romero. He turned to the right, walked up the river bank, and took the path to the ford. He stood there some moments, obviously measuring the volume of the flood with his eye, then he wheeled about, and struck into the wood in the direction of Puerto la Mar.

" Thou dost not need to publish thy reasons on the walls of the Padre Martinez's bodega," said Inez, aloud. Juan Romero could not walk to Puerto la Mar in less than two hours. He would remain there some time, — say one hour. If he walked back, he could not return under five hours' time; but stay! Why did people go to Puerto la Mar? It was usually for supplies of some kind. In that case, he would ride home. Was he going for supplies? she asked herself. As Juan Romero disappeared in the wood, Inez withdrew her gaze, and again fastened it upon the little clearing across the river. She had not to wait long for developments. A man emerged from the doorway of the casa. His gait was unsteady. He walked warily down to the bank of the river, and, lying down by the muddy flood, quite regardless of its color, he bathed his head and drank of the water, eagerly. Then he laved his feet. It was Tres Pelos.

After Inez had given the children their breakfast, and had left them in the care of Señorita, she again climbed to her vantage point. "It is early yet," she thought; "but surprises often come." And one came at that very moment. Along the path from Puerto la Mar she saw a white horse approaching, and, upon the horse, sat Juan Romero. On either side of the jaded animal hung a demijohn.

"Aha!" said Inez, in Spanish, "Juan Romero is willing to spend the money then. One cannot borrow the white horse of the innkeeper Valero. That I am sure of. Pay he must, and pay well. Aha! the kind Juan Romero. He loves the outcast Tre' Pelo'. He will give him, at his own expense, the fine rum, which he must buy with his hard-earned Mexican dollars. He will pay them over the counter to the Scotch thief Dugaldo. That is a millstone that one can see through as if it were glass. Oh! ta la!"

When next Tres Pelos came forth from the house, he was reeling. The following day, watch as Inez would, she could not discover that Tres Pelos had left the house at all. The river was

falling a little each hour; but Don Paul came
not to the ford. Alvarez, Don Paul's black
groom, came down early in the morning for some
limes. He reported to Inez that Don Paul was
ill with the calentura, that he could not leave
his bed. He came home soaked to the skin
three days ago.

"He loses his head at times," said Alvarez.
"He speaks about the mortgage," — every one
knows every one's else affairs in the vicinity of
Haldez, — "he says that his money is lost; that
the mortgage will never be paid now; but we
all know that the Señor Don Paul went to pay
the Alcalde three days ago."

"The Señor has paid his mortgage," said Inez,
decidedly. "I saw him pay it with these eyes.
I could see with no other eyes." This pleonasm
carried much weight with Alvarez. Even Inez
sometimes hit upon the truth. "He paid it to
the Alcalde in the store of Dugaldo, the white
Scotch thief, at three o'clock on Wednesday
last. I myself have been a witness to it."

"The saints above be praised!" Alvarez
ejaculated his words with fervency. It meant
less weeding round the banana mats.

"Tell the Señor Don Paul that the river has
not fallen at all."

"That would be an untruth, Inez, as you well
know."

"Oho!" screamed Inez, in a sudden rage. "You, half-blind, half-idiot, tell to me who live on the bank of the Rio Frio now these six years, that I cannot tell when the river falls, and when it rises. Did I not sit up there in the rafters one entire night?" What this question had to do with the facts of the present day, Alvarez was not bright enough to determine. "I tell you it has not fallen a single inch. Ask the Señor Don Paul if I may bring the children up to La Paciencia to-day. If the water rises more, I will arrive by four o'clock. Luis is away, and I am afraid." Inez's manner showed no fear, neither did her voice. Alvarez wondered at it, as he peered with his near-sighted eyes over the edge of the bank. Inez twitched him back by the rag hanging from his shoulder. "I tell you that I know all — everything — about the river, and you, ungrateful pig! will leave the poor Don Paul waiting for a taste of the lime-water while you stay to argue with me. Caramba hombre! These are the freshest; carry them quickly, and tell the Señor Don Paul that they are from the tree that the Old Señora, who is now with the saints in heaven, planted when he was a little boy." Inez sighed. "We were both children then."

Inez sighed again. She may have had aspirations, for all things are possible in the vicinity

of Haldez, but Don Paul had never been more
than kind to her, and Luis owned a small farm
where he raised a little tobacco. Well, what
would you have? Those ideas were forgotten
long ago, and Inez gave a sigh as she remembered them. The Old Señora had always a smile
for the pretty octoroon; perhaps she would not
have been so kind if, — and had not Don Paul
forgiven Luis the price of the banana patch
when he found that he was to marry Inez?
Otherwise how could she and the children have
lived? The dear Old Señora! dead now these
three years. People said that she walked. She
had been seen here, and there, and everywhere.
But Inez was not afraid; she would have welcomed the sight of the Old Señora, gladly. It
was said that she only appeared to evil-doers;
therefore, Inez argued, she was sure that she
never should see her. She needed no warning.
Perhaps — The sound of Alvarez's shuffling
feet recalled her to her surroundings.

"And be sure you keep the Señor quiet in
bed; you know how the calentura got on to the
brain of the shoemaker from Saltona, — not that
our Don Paul needs to be mentioned in the same
breath with the shoemaker from Saltona;" but
Alvarez had vanished.

That afternoon Inez and the three little ones
appeared at La Paciencia. Little Luis walked

beside the bull upon which Inez and the smaller children rode. Francesca patted the bull; Laura cried, as usual. The front view of the little Laura was never anything but a chasm.

"I may leave them here, may I not, Don Paul? Where should I expect kindness if not from the Demarisis?"

Don Paul smiled, and tried to nod acquiescence. The day was a scorching one, but Don Paul was covered with blankets, and the bed on which he lay shook under him.

"When the fever comes again," whispered Sarita, "what shall we do then? There is not a breath of air to-day, and my poor muchachito will suffer so much." Sarita, who had brought up the Old Señora, looked upon Don Paul as a little boy. "Alvarez tell me that the river fall very fas'." At these words Don Paul moved uneasily.

"The river falls, the river falls," he whispered. "Where is Tres Pelos?"

Inez turned upon Sarita with rage.

"The river falls! That is that blockhead Alvarez's sayings. It rises, I tell you, else why do I bring my children to take refuge at La Paciencia? It rises steadily. It will soon be up to the floor of my house."

"Then it is safe yet," muttered Don Paul. "I need not go yet."

"I must return to get some clothes, Sarita. If you know what is good for the calentura, you will keep the Señor Don Paul in his bed."

"I thank you, Inez; I know my business."

"If it were not for the rising of that river, I would stay, and — "

"I see de stones by de ole ford," remarked little Luis. Don Paul started up in his bed, wild, excited. A sharp slap from Inez sent Luis flying out through the doorway, — her premium on truth.

"Stones by the ford! This boy needs the glasses, Don Paul. I am very much worried about him; he sees all wrong. I tell you the river has risen a foot since morning. I must hurry back." And then to Sarita: "Keep those imbeciles away from the Señor Don Paul, and, if I can, I shall return to-night. If I do not come, understand that I have gone to the old Cabaña on the rising ground near Mercedes river patch. I am no fool, Sarita," nor was she.

As Inez passed the sitting-room door, she looked in. No one was there. She took a few steps past, and then wheeled quickly, and, returning, she entered. The cupboard door was open, no one was in sight. She snatched from a shelf a fresh white sheet, and, turning her skirt up round her hips, she hastily pinned the sheet around them. Inez then hastened down

an unfrequented by-avenue, and disappeared in
the mango grove.   An on-looker would have said
that Inez was a thief, as well as a liar.   It is well,
if one must steal and lie, to do it to some purpose.

When Inez reached the river bank, the water
had subsided to a great degree.   She unlocked
her door, threw the sheet inside, then, hastily
relocking it, she proceeded up the river bank
to the ford.   She wondered where Luis could
be.   She hoped that, as he had remained away
so long, he would not return until to-morrow.
This would allow her to work her will during
the night, and would also give her a grievance,
which was a good thing to have, as through it
Luis would remain in subjection for, perhaps,
three months to come.   When Inez reached the
ford, she could, as little Luis had informed Don
Paul, see the stones.   The water was still muddy
and boiling between the stepping-stones.

Everything comes to him who waits, and Inez,
feeling the truth of this proverb, sat herself
down on the bank.   An hour passed by; the
water had fallen rapidly, and the rocks which
outlined the upper side of the ford were standing
out here and there.   Inez stood up, and gathered
her one skirt about her slim, yellow legs.   Had
Don Paul seen her as she stepped confidently
from rock to rock, he would have doubted her
statement that she had seldom crossed the river.

Arrived at the sand cove, Inez cautiously looked about. She saw no one. Instead of taking the open path along the river bank, she struck into the wood in the direction of the Demarisi Rancho. She stepped warily, watching on all sides, and, finally, came out on the hill at the back of the small structure. The shutter was flung wide open. Inez advanced cautiously until she was close to the opening. She heard a man's heavy breathing. She looked through the open square. A man was lying there in a hammock. He was sleeping heavily. The nature of that slumber no one could doubt. The man was Tres Pelos. His face was red and bloated; by his side stood a rough table; upon the table was a demijohn; by its side, an overturned glass. A stream of strong-smelling, yellow liquid had run along the table, and was dripping to the floor.

"Ah, ha! As I thought!" whispered Inez. "I said that Juan Romero need not publish his reasons." There was a heavy step on the veranda on the other side of the casa. Inez dropped lightly under the flooring between the pilotillos. The flooring was eight feet from the ground, the place dark and cool. Inez heard Juan Romero's heavy step on the flooring above her head.

"And for me to be hiding among the pilotillos! under the flooring! But the devil must

F

be fought with his own weapons. The rum was not for thee," said Inez, looking upward; "all the same thou wilt need something to steady thy nerves before to-morrow."

Juan Romero paused for a moment as if regarding the unconscious sleeper. Then Inez heard him chuckle to himself, a chuckle of low cunning. Then she heard the gurgle of liquor. He was refilling the glass against such time as Tres Pelos should partially awake from his drunken sleep and stretch out his hand for more. Inez heard Juan Romero turn and, leaving the room, descend the steps which led from the veranda in front of the casa to the ground. Peeping out from behind the steps, Inez saw him go down the hill toward the river. She ran round to the back, lightly climbed into the room where Tres Pelos was sleeping, and drank off the liquor in the glass.

"I thank thee, Juan Romero," said she; "I do not mind being of so much expense to so generous a gentleman." She then returned to keep her watch underneath the house. It was not long before she saw Juan Romero returning. He had in his hand a long stick; it was a branch which he had been to the river bank to cut. There it was easy to find one to suit his purpose, though the fruit trees around the house did not furnish the kind that he wished. Some of the wild growths of the tropical forest take various shapes and forms. The stick that Juan Romero had in his hand had a well-curved end like a hook. "Bieng, bieng!" Inez whispered, "that will catch nicely in the string. Thou hast a fine mind, Juan Romero; a very fine mind. Perhaps it will not be so steady a mind after to-night."

Juan Romero began to peel his stick. Inez watched him with great interest. She was in no hurry to go home. It was pleasant to have company, although her host was not aware of her presence. She hoped that Luis would return while she was away, and, finding her gone, proceed on his journey; she cared not whither. So long as he gave her the next few hours to herself, she was content. Juan Romero walked round the house and struck into the plantation. "Caramba hombre! Thy time is short. Only a few hours yet. And what would you have then?" Inez addressed the pilotillos for want of a more appreciative audience. "Even a thief of Juan Romero's description must eat. He goes to fetch the Don Paul's fine bananas for his supper. Perhaps he will even cut a twelve-hand bunch. The good God alone knows! Thieves do not stop at even twelve-hand bunches." Whereupon Inez mounted the front steps and, entering the casa, she ransacked the small cupboard in the living-room. From a shelf she took an empty bottle labelled "Fine Champagne." "How long ago the old Señor Don Pablo must have left that bottle there," she mused. Inez walked into the sleeping-room, and, paying no heed to the unconscious Tres Pelos, she filled the bottle from the demijohn. This she corked with her slim yellow thumb, ran out of the house and down the front steps, and so toward the river, keeping the small building between herself and the whereabouts of Juan Romero. She recrossed the stepping-stones with ease, and was soon in her own cabin. She placed the bottle upon the table. "And why not?" she asked of a large lizard which poked its nose down through the hatch. "Is not my Luis's Christian stomach as empty and craving as the stomach of the heathen over yonder? All I ask of you is this: shall it not be filled when rum is running like the river below there? Ah! could I but have found another bottle! However, I also wish Tre' Pelo' to sleep for some time yet. In that, Juan Romero and I are well agreed."

At one o'clock that night all the earth was wrapped in silence. Only the crowing of the cocks calling and answering each other every hour from one colonia to another broke the phenomenal stillness. The water was flowing much more gently than when Inez returned from The Rancho. The now shallow river slipped in a golden stream down to the sea, whose volume it had so generously swelled for the past two days. The stepping-stones stood out bare and glittering. The moon was bright. It had just arisen over the tops of the palms upon the eastern bank, and flooded the world. The banana leaves rustled now and then.

Inez had made her preparations early in the evening, and had sat upon her doorstep watching for the advent of the moon. How slow it was in appearing to-night! Would it never rise? As soon as it peered over the tree-tops Inez arose, and, carrying in her hand an earthen cup, she was soon at the ford, and, crossing hurriedly, she ensconced herself behind the great tree where Juan Romero had been cutting branches on the first day of the flood. She waited for a half hour, and was just thinking of starting on a journey of discovery when she heard footsteps. They came from the direction of the ford. She hardly breathed; she dared not move, so long as there was danger of being seen.

When Juan Romero reached the bank above the sand cove, he descended and walked boldly out upon the stepping-stones. Arrived at mid-stream, he halted and began to rake among the gravel at the bottom of the river. For this he used the hooked stick which Inez had seen him peeling in the afternoon. The muddy water prevented his seeing the bottom of the river. He could succeed only by sense of feeling.

"Seeing thee work is pastime to me," chuckled Inez. "Thou wilt return to branch-sawing tomorrow, and who will weep?" Juan Romero's search did not at first prove successful. Inez watched with anxiety. "Perhaps it was washed away," she whispered to the nightingale above her, the nightingale who was giving a concert worthy of the Metropolitan Opera House, utterly unnoticed by these moral and musical degenerates. Inez leaned out from behind her tree. She saw Juan Romero get down from his rock and stand on the river bed. He dragged and scraped his hook along the bottom. He was in the water up to his middle, and your native, though he loves to bathe, grudges soaking his suit of clothes, for it is often his only one. As Juan Romero drew his hook from left to right it met with resistance. Inez watched him excitedly. Ah! what was that? Could it be the bag? "Work on," cried Inez, excitedly. "Work on. I shall reap all the benefit." Now was Inez's moment. She dipped her hand into the cup which she held. She filled it with the precious flour, so light and white, which she had bought at a fabulous price from her enemy Dugaldo. She covered her hair and face until she was unrecognizable. She coughed and spluttered, but Juan Romero was too intent upon his prize to hear anything.

From under her skirt Inez drew the sheet, and wrapped it round her tall form. She then stepped swiftly down to the sand cove. Juan Romero's back was toward her. He was tugging at some heavy, resisting weight. Ah! there it comes, up, up! He raised the stick with difficulty; his motion a hand-over-hand one. A large leathern bag appeared in view, intact, unopened, just as it had been when it had slipped from Don Paul's shoulder into the boiling flood. Juan Romero could not forbear a shout. There was no one near but Tres Pelos, and he was lying in a drunken stupor. He raised the heavy weight in his aching arms.

"That is as it should be, Juan Romero," said Inez. "Do all the work, and I will have all the play." He had just laid the bag of silver upon the large flat stone, when a shrill, soul-curdling yell broke the midnight stillness. Juan Romero's blood froze. He turned. The sight which met his gaze caused him to start. He tottered, lost his footing, and fell backward. With a shriek of "The Old Señora!" his head sank below the muddy waters. Fright so utterly unnerved him that his strength was gone. He was swept down the river, catching here and there at a slippery rock, only to lose his grasp again. When he recovered himself and arose from the water, where he had been rolled over and over and filled with a solution of mud, he waded with difficulty to the shore. The bank was steep, and covered with slimy moss and soaked leaves. He stumbled along in the lonely night, hardly daring to look toward the ford. When at last he reached it and sought his spoil, the stepping-stone was bare! Inez heard his hoarse cry as he clutched at the place where he had laid the treasure. "Let us hope that thou art drowning," she said, as she tugged and dragged the leathern bag along the lonely path.

The following morning Inez went to La Paciencia for her children. The little Laura, who had been enjoying life to the utmost, because for a day she had known where she was to get her next meal, cried, on principle, as soon as she saw her mother. Her feelings were, though she could not put them into words: "She says that I never do anything but cry; I will not disappoint her."

Little Luis asked: "Well, and was not the ford so dry that you could see the stone, madre?"

"It was dry! thou wert right for once, child." Luis himself came from the kitchen. "Thou ingrate! Where hast thou been? Leaving thy poor wife to keep the house while thou amusest thyself and spendest all thy little earnings at the gambling house of Pedro Bolero!" This was a fine stroke. Luis looked down, and remained at home for many weeks after. Then Inez found her way into Don Paul's bedroom. He looked thin and pale. Sarita had propped him up in bed, where he lay with a sad smile on his face.

"What is that, Inez? some more limes?" Inez placed the heavy parcel on the bed beside her dear Don Paul. He looked earnestly at the familiar thing. His eyes grew large; he clutched at the bag. "Where? where? who?"

"It is indeed your moggage, Señor Don Paul," said Inez, smiling. "I must inform you, Señor, that I do not consider Tre' Pelo' a very first-class looker."

WILLIE BAKER'S GOOD SENSE

WILLIE BAKER'S GOOD SENSE

MISSER WILLIAMS, the young American who had come over from San Fedro to Las Lilas as manager, needed funds with which to pay his workmen. He had come down from the north to take charge of the great sugar estate of San Fedro, on the shores of the sea, at the urgent request of its owner, and having arranged matters and set the owner upon his feet again, Misser Williams was going home to the States.

Señora Sagasta, at Las Lilas, had heard of Misser Williams's knowledge of ledgers and international law, and the rights of foreigners, as well as of his knowledge of cacao and banana culture, and of human nature as exemplified in the native. The Señora remembered that she was but a woman when she thought of the ledgers and banana culture, and that she had a slight claim upon the name of foreigner — her grandmother had been an American — when she thought of international law and the control of half a hundred peons, and she decided that just at that time Misser Williams was the one man in the world for her. It is but just to say that her wishes were not colored by sentiment. She had never seen Misser Williams when she invited him to come to Las Lilas as manager.

The Señora reasoned thus: " The peons will always overreach a poor weak woman, and a native manager will connive at their misdoings." She saw that the plantation had been steadily going down hill since the Señor Sagasta's death, but how to set it right she did not know. The Señora Sagasta was not very clever at figures; her books were in a rather confused state.

When Misser Williams opened the large ledger, he thought that it was upside down, until he turned it round and opened from the other end. Then he found if you began from that end, that the ledger was also upside down. The truth seemed to be that Lola, the Señora's maid, who arranged the library and " oficina," and dusted the books, and tore up any papers which had writing on them, turned the great ledger over and round every day when she dusted; and the Señora opened it as it lay, back, front, right, or wrong side up, and made her entries in her nice pointed Spanish hand, — entries such as

" Paid Aroya seven Mexicans in advance."

"Lent Pedrito seven pounds of white sugar and ten pounds of rice for his mother."

"Bought a mantilla de silla for the white bull."

"Paid Señor Canuda 1.50 Mex.; owe him 4.75."

Added to these entries, Misser Williams found the books scrawled full of recipes, — for hot soups and sin coches,[1] as well as careful instructions in the matters of fancy work and crocheting. Between two pages filled with the most intricate memoranda as to moneys recently paid to 'Cito Mores, the manager, he discovered a crochet needle, some blue wool patted flat, and the beginning of something unintelligible to his mind, which the Señora called "shells." When the Señora told Misser Williams that Aroya had worked out the time for which she had paid him seven Mexicans in advance, he said that he could find no trace of it. Recipes he found in abundance; receipts were few. When he asked her how Pedrito had paid for the sugar and rice which she had lent him, she replied that "it was a small matter. Would he have the old woman starve? Those were not Island manners."

When he looked over the items with regard to the purchase of the aparejo cover, and asked for the receipt, she replied that she was afraid that Lola had burned it; that Lola seemed to

[1] A stew of beef, vegetables, cereals, and what not.

think that she must always burn the scraps with the writing on them. "And I cannot convince her otherwise," added the Señora, helplessly. "But I paid him the 4.75 last Thursday," declared the pretty widow. "It was only the receipt for the first payment that was lost."

"Then you have the second?"

"No; he assured me that it made no difference, and that he could not write with my pen."

"Where is your pen, Señora?"

The Señora walked to the large upright desk and cupboard combined which had been the Señor Sagasta's. She drew the holder away from the door where the pen-point had been thrust to keep it closed. Misser Williams looked critically at the pen.

"All men have their limitations," said he; "the Señor Canuda is no exception."

When the store-keeper came to be paid for the aparejo cloth, the Señora had no proof that he had already received his money; so that six dollars and twenty-five cents of good Mexican silver changed place for the second time from the Señora's long purse to Canuda's longer pocket. Misser Williams was not many days in discovering that this was the principle upon which the plantation at "Las Lilas" was run.

"Seems to me that's a very expensive aparejo cloth, Señora," said Misser Williams.

The Señora tossed her small, well-shaped head.

"I am one who like the things of the most expensive, Señor; and if I command a fine red cloth as a cover to my saddle, what is that to any one? The red color makes the white bull *très gai*," — the Señora had been educated in Paris. "All would be dull and sombre if my aparejo cover were as dark as my gown." The Señora looked down at the black skirt in which she mourned for the defunct Sagasta. "My days are dull enough, Señor. Would you have me always sad? Must there be no brightness in my life, — not even a red saddle-cloth?"

"God forbid!" Misser Williams ejaculated the words with fervency. "Buy all the saddle-cloths that you please, Señora, but don't let us pay for them twice."

"But that is the reason of the wealth of the Señor Canuda," argued the Señora, as if she considered it a virtue. "Every one understands the Señor's ways; he is always double-paid. Do you not suppose, Señor, that I knew very well that I should have to pay him nine or eleven dollars for my aparejo cover? He told me five dollars Mexican when first I ordered it, but I very well knew that I should have to pay more than twice that sum before he had done."

"You won't again, Señora." Misser Williams

G

was scrutinizing the ledger with a look of utter helplessness.

"And how then is the poor man to live?"

Misser Williams broke into a laugh over the Señora's inconsequence.

"Your books are in a hopeless muddle, Señora. You do, indeed, need some one to take care of you — your plantation."

The Señora cast down her eyes, — those large, Spanish eyes. She thought of the time to come, when she should have lightened her mourning enough to tuck a rose amid the tresses of her blue-black hair, just above her small ear.

Perhaps it was natural that when first he came among them, the peons did not like Misser Williams overmuch. He knew their ways, and temporized with none of them. And, because of his long stay at San Fedro, he was able to read a man's character almost at once. A good servant he thoroughly appreciated; a shiftless or deceitful worker he marked, and never forgave.

"None of your Don Juan's or Don Tomaso's for me," he said. "My name is John Thomas Williams. You can call me Mr. Williams, or you can let it alone."

Those peons who could not manage "Misser Williams" addressed him as Don Jack-Tom, which they considered a wonderful achievement, and which he chuckled over as a victory for himself. It was natural that the peons did not look with affection upon a manager who had made such radical changes as Misser Williams had compassed at Las Lilas. Now, the Señora did not pay over a quarter more than she should have done. Now, there was no advancing money for work promised, but never performed. Now, there were no pesos given out for ointment for the backs of the numerous bulls, — pesos which had been paid over the counter at Padre Martinez's bodega for salve of one kind or another for the peons' interior. Now, there was no unnecessary expenditure for a pick or a machete to replace a broken article.

"Bring me the two pieces," was the order nowadays. Misser Williams was firm. No money should be expended for a new article until the old one had been delivered at the repairing shed.

"Very hard times now, at Las Lilas," said 'Cito Mores, "since Don Jack-Tom come down. It must be painful, indeed, to dwell in so honest a country as his! In what way do the poor working people support themselves?"

Misser Williams's care of Las Lilas included the care of the Señora, and we usually learn to love those who are dependent upon us.

The day had come for Misser Williams to

go to Puerto la Mar for his monthly money. Since the Señor Sagasta's death, the Señora had been obliged to send 'Cito Mores with a draft; and the sum for which she drew had usually dwindled much by the time that she received her bags of silver dollars. Sometimes the bank had asked a large commission, sometimes 'Cito Mores had been obliged to procure the money of Dugaldo, who kept the best store in the town, and he had charged a larger commission than even the bank. There are all grades of thieves! Sometimes 'Cito Mores lost a bag of dollars on his way home, or declared that he had. Always, after these excursions, 'Cito Mores seemed to enjoy life to the full; to attend all cock-fights, to bet money, and spend generously upon himself; but there was no proof of wrong-doing, and no redress. Naturally, 'Cito Mores did not approve of the advent of Misser Williams.

"They will steal no more of your money, Señora," said the new manager.

Late one afternoon, he started for Puerto la Mar. He was to ride down to the coast, try to cash his draft at the bank, or at Dugaldo's. If not successful there, then he must cross the bay to Saltona, and go to Cespedes, that honorable man, who would not take from him more than treble commission.

"I shall get off easily, even so," thought Misser Williams.

"You will first take the black coffee with me, on the veranda, Señor Managero."[1]

"I have not the time, Señora."

"Not the time!" The Señora was not accustomed to having her attentions refused. "You will at least play for me the pretty French song, 'Bonjour, Suzon'? That song which I heard Faure himself sing so long ago in Paris. That song *Which — I — Love*." The words were separated and emphasized. The Señora's name was Suzon.

"I cannot stay even for that. I have a long ride before me, Señora. I am late, as it is."

The Señora pouted. She was lovely at twenty-three. She raised her shapely hand toward the bougainvillea vine which clambered over the veranda, there was no rose bush near. Should she? Ah, yes. Why not? We can live only once; let us live while we are young. The Señora had never lived at all. Simple existence had been her portion. The Señor Sagasta had been seventy-three when her mother had married her to him. She plucked the rich purple-red bloom, and tucked it behind her ear. She drew back the dainty black muslin, and

---

[1] It is quite a common custom to give an English word a Spanish termination.

showed the fluted flounce beneath; also the small black slipper and the white stocking, so dear to the feminine Spanish soul. Misser Williams was adamant.

"The roan, Pedrito!" said he. "A' Dios Señora."

"And you will not play for me? It is not much! I have had so little pleasure — till now."

Misser Williams stopped short in his descent of the steps. Was it the tone of her voice or the words "I have had so little pleasure — till now"? Ah! "*Till now.*" The color suffused his face.

"You will play for me?"

Ah! who could resist her? He turned quickly and came up the steps and entered the room which gave upon the veranda. He took his cornet from the nail where it hung, and, coming out, he stood near her hammock and put the shining metal to his lips; and then he poured forth the mellow notes of the gay French song. And she, as she sat upright in her hammock, tapped the black slipper against the boards in time to the music. Her scarlet shawl trailed upon the floor; her scarlet pillow lay there ready for her shapely head; the bougainvillea flower hung over her delicate ear. One large curl drooped nearly to her eyes; a comb stood up high at the back of her head. It was too warm for the mantilla, which, however, lay there ready, — all so suggestive of sunny Spain.

"Bonjour, Suzon," he played, "Bonjour, Suzon."

Pedrito led the horse to the foot of the steps.

"A flower for your buttonhole, Señor." She arose and approached him.

She picked a second blossom from the bougainvillea vine. The bract showed purple in her hand. He took the curious bloom from her; their fingers touched for the first time.

"I prefer the red one; I will exchange with you," he said.

The manager held the blossom toward her. She hesitated, and stretched her hand a third time toward the vine.

"No, no!" he said. "Not that one."

Again she hesitated for a moment; and then, swiftly, as if to forestall repentance, she snatched the flower from behind her ear, thrust it into his hand, and dashed away to her hammock. He put spurs to the roan, and as he disappeared between the rows of banana trees, she heard him whistling softly the strains of "Bonjour, Suzon." Sometimes the sound was muffled, as if it came through the petals of a flower.

Mamma Cordeza emerged from the sitting-room door, — a withered old crone who had been much more beautiful at twenty-three than was her daughter; indeed, she had been more beautiful at thirty. And now, at forty-five, she was an old woman; but the waning of her charms had not affected her heart, soul, spirit, thought, mind, or dreams,—she was young in all of these. Ah! if only we could appear as we feel, with what youthful and beautiful creatures would the world be peopled! The shrivelled casket, known as the old Señora, held a youthful and still aspiring soul. People had thought that the Señor Sagasta was courting the mother, and lo! it was the young daughter whom he had married, over there at the little church at Haldez.

"Are you then giving encouragement to that young man, Suzon?"

"I am encouraging him to go to Puerto la Mar for me, mamma, to obtain the money with which to pay these clamorous peons."

"Tut, tut"—or the Spanish equivalent for *tut, tut*—"you very well know what I mean."

"I do not know what you mean, mamma; I doubt very much if you yourself know what you mean."

"Are you thinking of marrying again, Suzon?"

"No, madre mia; I am much too happy as I am."

"And, in truth, I should forbid the banns." What a kind ally was the old Señora for Misser Williams, if he only knew it! Opposition, in some cases, is our very best friend.

"I am twenty-one, mamma."

"And much over!" snapped the old Señora.

"Every year added to my age, madre mia, adds one to yours, also. You married me once, mamma; I am Señora now, you no longer have any voice in my affairs."

The old Señora could not believe her shriv-elled brown ears. The Señora Sagasta arranged her pillow comfortably, — that scarlet pillow which so well became her dark beauty. She allowed the scarlet shawl to trail a trifle more upon the floor; she pulled her comb a little higher, and her curl a little lower; then she raised the black skirt an inch, showing an added bit of slipper-tip. She surveyed herself in the long glass, which was fitted into a panel of the veranda, — a very satisfactory dress rehearsal. Where was that bougainvillea flower? Ah, yes! just peeping forth from the opening in her dress. She arose and placed the bract in a vase of fresh water, and raised the vase to her nose. The bougainvillea has little odor, but the nose is just above the lips. After this she held another dress rehearsal.

When Misser Williams arrived at Puerto la Mar, the night had fallen. He could not pro-cure his money there; there were not five hun-dred pesos in the place. He must go further.

"I cannot cash the Señor's draft," said

Dugaldo. "My boat crosses when the breeze serves, early in the morning. The Señor can go over in her."

"Who sails her?" asked Misser Williams.

"Willie Baker; he is a good man."

"Who else? I am bringing the Señora's money back with me."

"Two new men, to be sure! but I fancy they are all right. The Señor can sleep in my house on the wharf, and be ready to sail when the wind comes. Cespedes will cash a draft of any size."

The house upon the wharf was anything but a luxurious abode; rats ran riot, lizards squeaked, and an occasional lively splash underneath the boards where he lay reminded Misser Williams of the probable vicinity of that scavenger of the sea. — the shark. He was glad when morning came, and Willie Baker declared himself ready to start. The fin-keel was a fine craft; she had been built for Dugaldo "at a place, somewhere near the north pole, named Marble-a-head." She made her trip in five or six hours.

Cespedes willingly cashed the Señora's draft, charging the usual exorbitant commission, because there was no possibility of competition. The bags of silver dollars were carried down to the boat by Cespedes's trusty men, — four bags in all, — and were thrown into the bottom of the craft.

"The land breeze serves at midnight," said Cespedes. "Have you trustworthy men?"

"I have never heard of anything happening since that affair of the English agent; beside, I have Willie Baker at the tiller."

"I suppose he is a good man," said Cespedes, somewhat doubtfully.

At one o'clock a gentle breeze came wafting down from the vega. The light, which heralded the moon's approach, shone softly in the eastern sky; but, as yet, the only light of practical use was the lantern at the masthead of the *Paloma*, and the hundred or more cucullas which flew about Misser Williams's head, or crawled upon his coat, his sleeve, his hand, or burrowed in his hair, and showed each his embarrassment of lights, — two at the head, and one underneath the body. Misser Williams caught a half dozen and confined them under an overturned water-glass, and then lay down on the deck to examine his accounts by their brilliant glow. The frogs croaked within the marsh of the vega, an occasional fish splashed his silver drops upward in a wide-spreading bow, the scented, spicy breeze blew softly across his face, the waves tap-tapped the sides of the boat with short, sharp, little slaps, calling, "Look over the side — the side — look over the side — the side — the side — at my oblong pattern of blue — of blue, of blue and brown — of blue and brown."

And then the moon came sailing gorgeously over the crest of the hill, and it was light as day.

Misser Williams lifted the water-glass and allowed the dazed cucullas to go free. Looking out to sea, he could distinguish the distant islands at the mouth of the grand bay on which he sailed; turning his gaze upon the shore near by, it rested upon a panoramic scene composed of straggling rows of houses, gleaming white in the brilliant light, 'neath tufts of palm leaves which topped, each one, its tall, straight shaft.

Misser Williams lay almost in the land of dreams. The whispering of the breeze, the caressing of its soft fingers, carried him away in thought across twenty miles of land and water, to a casa where the bougainvillea grew, and where other and softer fingers were, perhaps, waiting to clasp his own. Yes, he would care for her, he was caring for her now; her interests were his. Why else should he have taken this fatiguing trip to bring to her the money that she needed? With a start, he turned and looked down into the cockpit. José 'Manuel was standing below there, and staring at the great canvas bags, as he leaned against the framework of the boat. The glittering gipsy look in the eye told a clear tale of avarice and desire. José 'Manuel glared fixedly at the bags, Misser Williams watched José 'Manuel, and Delande, the Frenchman, watched Misser Williams. How easy it would be, thought José 'Manuel; only a quick stab, the sliding of an inanimate body over the side, where the sharks swam thickest. Then, up sail, up helm, and away to some outlying island, and, from there, an escape to civilized lands and life! life! life! No work ever again! Misser Williams's intent look hypnotized José 'Manuel, and brought his eyes upward from the bags, to meet the clear, gray gaze of the young American.

" That won't work, José; think again."

José 'Manuel shrugged his shoulders, and turned his back on Misser Williams. He looked across the white deck, out to the water. It rippled in green and gold discs, — beautiful and brilliant. Lap — lap — lap — slap-dash, as the bow of the boat raised up on an unsubdued swell which would not down, though the land breeze was blowing a counter current across it.

Delande looked searchingly at José 'Manuel. He, Delande, had the jib-sheet in his hand. Suppose that he paid off, and Willie Baker, the half-breed, agreed to sail for the open sea; but he was in the bow, and Willie Baker sat stolidly at the tiller.

" José 'Manuel, get up in the bow."

José 'Manuel climbed up and sat down by Delande. Misser Williams took a long step toward the stern of the boat.

"Willie Baker, it's you and I against those two. They mean to kill me if they can. Watch them, Willie Baker! and let me know the moment that they start, either one, for the cockpit. When your father came down from Charleston and settled at Saltona, he little thought that the time would come when you would have the chance to protect one of his own countrymen."

Willie Baker turned his eyes on the two men in the bow. José 'Manuel was talking in a low tone to Delande. The language was a patois, probably unintelligible even if distinguishable. The men bent each his gaze upon the deck. Neither one made a gesture which could be construed into meaning anything hostile.

"It wouldn't be worth your while, Willie Baker. There isn't enough to divide among three, and you are sure to get caught. Do you remember Desborde and Plon? To be sure, they sent the English agent to the sharks, but the English Company marched them up before the Alcalde one fine morning, and in ten minutes the Alcalde marched them up before a platoon of soldiers, — perhaps it was fifteen minutes. I know that the soldiers had to be awakened and have time to load their carbines. I wouldn't try it, Willie Baker; I wouldn't, really."

"Don' go try nuttin'."

"That's right, Willie Baker. Your word's as

good as your bond, and both are worthless; but you have some common sense, — horse sense, — and the stocks are not at all pleasant." Willie Baker looked ruefully at his black legs. "The stocks you may get out of, but," Misser Williams nodded across at the white town which shone out clear in the moonlight, "those men at Saltona get very tired when business is dull. They don't shoot very straight, but, my God! I had rather face the sharks than their bungling," Misser Williams shuddered, "they take so long at it."

"Reckon Misser Williams raight."

"I'm dead tired, Willie Baker. I won't say good-night; I don't mean to sleep. I shall hear the moment you call."

Most of us are unintentional liars. Misser Williams unbuckled his belt, took his pistol in his right hand, and, descending into the cockpit, laid down with his head upon one of his bags, and in the space of five seconds was in a sleep so heavy that no dreams even of the Señora Sagasta disturbed him. How long his slumber lasted, he did not know. He was partly aroused by a shout. He struggled to awake. He heard a heavy splash. A second shot was followed by the sound of grinding, grating feet overhead. Coarse oaths, a scream of rage and pain, and then a second splash finished the combat. He tugged at his heavy eyelids with numb fingers. He looked upward to the great vault overhead. The boat was yawing round. The North Star was now upon his right; it should have been upon his left. He endeavored to speak. He was drunk with sleep, and made but an inaudible sound, at least to Willie Baker; and then he raised himself to a sitting posture, and, gathering his slow-returning strength, he shouted, —

"It all raight, Misser Williams." It was Willie Baker's voice.

Misser Williams stood up.

"Dat dam tiller, he gif a heap o' trouble. Got to git de jib-sheet."

"Jib-sheet? Where's José 'Manuel?"

Willie Baker nodded over the side. "Reckon dey ain' much leff o' José by now. Dey make dere fus' co'se offen José."

"Man! What do you mean?"

"Seen 'em comin' fo' you, Misser Williams; fus' one cropin' long f'om de bow, den de remainin' one. *Had* to fix 'em. Shaaks mighty glad! José 'Manuel fus' co'se; Delande, he green enough to come along in time fo' de salad. No use talkin', we'se los' dere suvices! Me an' you got to git dis dam fin-keel into po't somehow. She drif'ed down to leward now putty consid'able."

JONES'S NEW FIN-KEEL

JONES'S NEW FIN-KEEL

Don Carlos Winton had come over from Caño Sandros in Jones's new fin-keel. He had come to meet Madam Winton, and he went to Flandreau's hotel to wait until the steamer should arrive.

Flandreau lived by making pipes and anarchy. The pipes had brought him in a good bit of late; anarchy had not been so lucrative, for Flandreau now lived in a town where social anarchy was first nature and not at all a paying business, only nature. In Chicago, in the old days, anarchy had brought in to Flandreau a tidy little sum; when he met and conspired according to orders.

Flandreau was a short, shiny, round-faced conspirator, *nez retroussé*, mouth broad, and always smilingly open, showing a tooth and a half in front. Flandreau kept the hotel at Andaluze, and Totty was supposed to help him.

Totty was dark and slim — dark for a white woman, light for a negress; she was, perhaps,

a fair sort of octoroon.   Her hair was wavy
and soft and very dark; one of her sweet eyes
was brown, the other blue.   The blue eye had
a slight — a very slight — cast, always a taking
feature.   Totty's hands were long and slim and
helpless-looking, like their owner.   She dragged
herself slowly across the floor of the tiny sitting-
room and laid the table for breakfast.   Each
step that Totty took she accompanied with a
sigh.

The door on the right of the sitting-room
opened into Totty's room.   Upon her bureau
stood a picture of her handsome white father,
"Misser Thompson, of Gainesville, up No'th."
Beside the portrait stood a brandy bottle which
seldom contained its proper amount of the potent
revivifier, because that quality belonged in a
measure to Totty herself.   Near these articles
were Totty's hair-brush and the butter for breakfast.   The crackers, a great delicacy, were kept
in a tin box under Totty's bed.

At the back of the sitting-room opened two
doors, one into the single guest chamber which
the house afforded, the other into the kitchen.
These rooms comprised the hotel.   A narrow
veranda ran along the front of the house.   A
step down and two onward led you to the little
whitewashed gate.   The house was also whitewashed.   Battens nailed over the wide cracks

kept out the tropical rains. Before the open-
ings which served for windows, heavy board
shutters, painted blue, hung slopingly upon rusty
or broken hinges. Inside the house, running up
the walls and across the ceiling, were the brown-
covered pathways of the comajens, who made
their nests upon the roof; large black excres-
cences were these, looking like great fungi.

Señor Winton had come over from Caño
Sandros to meet the Clyde steamer — " Vapor
Cleede," Flandreau called it. By this boat
Señor Winton expected his mother, and he had
engaged the entire hotel for her. She was to
sleep in the one bedroom which the house
afforded, and Señor Winton was to sleep in a
cot in the front room, which was drawing-room,
bedroom, and dining-room combined. If the
table was pushed close against the back wall,
the cot could be squeezed in. But as this pro-
cedure practically closed the kitchen door, Señor
Winton could not think of retiring until the
other inmates had settled down for the night.

Señor Winton had some big bags of silver
dollars and some small bags of gold. He had
drawn the money that morning at Francoli's.
He put the bags down behind the bed which
had been prepared for Madam Winton, and
went out to learn if the steamer had been
sighted. It was very early in the morning.

Flandreau had been up to the top of the hill which rose before the house. He sat under a cabbage palm and whiled away the time by carving a pipe which Señor Winton had ordered. Flandreau was putting a finishing touch to his pipe when he thought it wise to raise his eyes; this caused him to raise his round little body.

"Aaah! 'Vapor Cleede!'" said Flandreau.

He gazed, as he spoke, out toward the ocean. There, among the buttons of islands which dot the foam-capped surface of the mouth of the great bay, he perceived a faint line of smoke. The trade wind was carrying this smoke into the bay ahead of the incoming steamer. Flandreau did not reseat himself. He descended the hill, cutting and polishing as he went. He did not halt nor stumble as he walked down the uneven way, worn by hard black soles among the scorched and slippery grass. He put his round jovial face in at the doorway of the sitting-room and announced "Vapor Cleede," much as a butler announces us to our friends. Señor Winton, who had not gone high enough up the hill and had returned disappointed, arose.

"Wait breakfast then, Totty, until the Señora arrives."

"I wait," sighed Totty. She patiently removed the butter from the breakfast table and replaced it upon the bureau in her bedroom, pushing back the brush with the edge of the plate. This seemed to have been the only preparation thus far made for a morning meal.

"She not lonk vey off; come in time for early b'eakfas'," smiled Flandreau.

Totty arose with a patient sigh, dragged herself across the floor, and restored the butter to the table. There were hollows under Totty's pretty eyes, a heavier one under the blue eye than under the brown. That side of her face pained her the most. She had what she called a rising in her breast. She said that the doctor at Saltona was coming up next week to cut it away. Flandreau looked as near savage as possible at this, and put up his lip, this gentle anarchist, like a little child, ready to cry.

When "Vapor Cleede" was within a half hour of her time for anchoring, Señor Winton went out of the gate and down the rough path toward the custom house. He stopped there and informed the officer in charge that Madam Winton would soon arrive, and that the representative of the syndicate which collects the revenues had received a letter from those in control, saying that Madam's belongings were to be exempt, as nearly as possible, from duties.

"As the Señor Don Vintone says," returned that gracious gentleman, bowing low, and immediately made a mental note to raise the duty on the Señora's piano from twenty to thirty dollars Mexican.

This matter settled satisfactorily to the Señor Don Carlos Winton, he walked through the custom house and down to the wharf. There he took a small native boat, and rowing out to the steamer was soon on board. His negro boatmen were astonished at the ease with which he went up the rope thrown to him. Don Carlos had been the president of the athletic club at college, and " hand-over-hand " was play to him.

His ascent was watched with anxiety by Madam Winton, a blond, determined-looking woman, who had come down against the advice of all friends, including Winton himself, to spy out the land. She said, " To see how things are going," which meant in reality that she intended to " run " the plantation, and Charles and the entire island into the bargain. She had tried to run the Clyde steamer, but the mighty deep has its value in other ways beside commercial and social interchange between countries, and while billows rolled, and Vapeur Clyde wallowed, ideas were *nil*, and conversation languished.

" Charles, dear, take me away from this horrid place," said Madam Winton.

They pushed their way along the narrow deck. It was blockaded by a fat old negress from " The Cape." She was taking the tall young daughter of the banker to his house at Pradeau. The banker's daughter was quite dark, and notwithstanding her African features she was very pretty. Her eyes were blue, and her hair the color of copper. Such strange combinations and surprises does one see in the island. The banker's daughter spoke French and Spanish and a little Italian, but no English. She was fresh from her finishing school in Paris. The young girl who accompanied her, her sister, was of pure African type.

Far down below the deck, dipping and rocking upon the great swells as they came rolling in from the outer sea, was a long-boat. Madam Winton and her son could not pass this point, the crowd and obstructions being for the moment so great. They cast their eyes downward at the boat as it rocked on the waves, and then were aware that the shrill screams from the old negress beside them were directed to some one below. Beside the two oarsmen the boat contained three women. One of the women was gazing upward at the aged crone, and they found that she was the mark for the old woman's shrill words.

" Yaas ; Iah see youah mudda day fo' Iah leff. Youah mudda he healthy ; youah mudda he fat as pig. Fat as pig ? He fat as hog, fat hog ! Youah mudda try sen' some peyah [pear],

aguacate peyah. Him luk an' luk all ober,
youah mudda do, but he ain' fin' no aguacate
peyah. Oh! youah mudda fat; youah mudda
healt'y; youah mudda fat as —"

"Charles! what are you stopping for? Do
get by."

Winton squeezed determinedly past, lowering
his eyes the while, not anxious that his mother
should discover that he had found the byplay
at all amusing. Rivers of warm water were
streaming down Madam Winton's face.

"Come up and have a glass of wine, Mr.
Winton." It was the captain's cheery voice.

"Charles, order your boat to the gangway
and get me ashore, away from these brutes."

"Thank you, captain, no! Poor mother! and
this is only the beginning!"

"Hombre! hombre!" called Madam Winton
to her son's boatmen, at the same time beckon-
ing them to approach the long ladder which had
now been lowered. Madam Winton knew some
tag-ends of various languages. She had tried
them upon the crew and the company's agents
as they came on board; on the stevedores and
the "Turk's Island Niggers," who had made the
voyage from their island. Happy, irresponsible,
smiling creatures, who worked all day and sang
all night. "Thank God! that I can speak English, blessed English, once again, Charles."

A peculiar smile overspread Winton's face. His sense of humor was keen. The smile might have been intended to conceal the thought that unless Madam Winton spoke English she would be dumb.

" Well, you'll have to, to me, mother," Señor Winton laughed.

She stepped on the grating.

" 'Way down there, in that little boat?"

" I'm sorry, mother."

Madam Winton started down the long, shaking, temporary ladder.

" Wait, madam ! " called the captain.

She was half-way down. She shook a determined head.

" I wait for no man, Charles."

Winton knew by experience that she never did. Time and tide were nothing to Madam Winton.

" Pull up closer, Peter," called Winton, anxiously.

The negro backed the stern in to the lower grating. Madam Winton descended majestically.

" Wait, madam, wait ! " Unheeding the breathless captain, who had run down the bridge ladder, Madam Winton stepped on the tread above the grating.

" Choose your time," warned the captain.

Too late! A wave from the consistent trade wind of Christoforo Colon rolled oilily up, its swelling surface a symphony of yellow and green. It grew to gigantic proportions as it reached Madam Winton; so she was convinced. Even her waist belt was wet. Back up the ladder she came.

"Down to first principles, Charles; I must have everything."

She dripped steaming into the hot cabin. In the saloon outside her stateroom door the steward and two assistants had just succeeded in pressing down and locking the gaping cover of her trunk. A queue of natives of all shades were streaming past the water-cooler, taking each his turn at the iced water, their luxury every two weeks, when Vapeur Clyde was in harbor.

"Open that trunk!"

Winton could not bear the look of despair on the faces of the servants. He vanished.

Madam Winton's second descent of the ladder was made under the wing of the experienced captain.

"Now jump!" And she landed dry, if a little wanting in dignity, in the stern of the boat, as it rose on the crest of watered silk.

It was a long day at Totty's.

"When can you have lunch?" demanded Madam Winton of the subdued Totty. It was then 7.45 A.M., and she had just finished breakfast.

"Not befo' nine o'clock, I reckon."

Totty sighed; Madam Winton sniffed; Winton laughed. Flandreau sat upon the veranda, carved the pipe, and sang softly to himself : —

> "Il avait un petit navire,
> Qu'il n'avait ja-ja-jamais navigué."

"Our case, I suspect, mother. You know we are to cross the bay at one o'clock to-night, in Jones's new fin-keel."

"Never!" said Madam Winton.

"Then you'll never go," replied her son.

Alternative between crossing the bay at one A.M. or remaining with Totty and Flandreau! To be sure, she might return to Vapeur Clyde, and so home again. When the horrors of the known weigh heavily upon our souls, the unknown opens up possibilities somewhat tempting.

A long, hot, weary day, during which Madam Winton rocked upon the veranda in a chair which Flandreau had made expressly for Totty, or else appeared in the kitchen, offering to help with the cooking. As there was nothing to cook, her offer was easily dispensed with.

"Seems to me she's dark for a white woman," hazarded Mrs. Winton.

"Yes," answered Charles.

Totty was pretending to pick some skinny birds which Winton had bought of a small negro. She sat on the kitchen steps and sighed. A gaunt shadow fell across the pan resting on her knees.

"Where did you marry your husband, — here, or in the States?"

Totty sighed.

"Ain' got no time to talk," said Totty. "Almighty sick!"

Madam Winton returned to Totty's chair.

"Where did you marry your wife?" she asked, as she swished herself into the chair, knocking Flandreau's pipes off the small bench and his tools upon the floor. Flandreau stooped to pick up the polisher.

"Haingh?" asked Flandreau.

"I asked where did you mar—"

"Mother, don't! He doesn't understand English very well." Which was true of Flandreau when he did not choose to understand it.

Madam Winton was awakened from the first uneasy snatch of sleep, which heat and mosquitoes had heretofore prevented.

"Is that you, Charles?"

"Yes, mother."

"I haven't had a wink of sleep the whole night."

Then it *was* the shutter, thought Winton. He would not voice his unfounded suspicions.

"Nor I, mother. I became convinced that all the mosquitoes in the island were inside of my netting, so I tied a string round the bottom and 'put 'em up in a bag,' like the man in Fourth Avenue with his bananas, and got outside."

A heavy footfall sounded upon the veranda floor.

"Moon soon be up, win' risin'; time to depart, Señor Don Carlos." It was Jones, from the fin-keel boat *La Madrugada*.

When Madam Winton was dressed, Winton reached down behind her bed and dragged out the heavy bags.

"Dear me! Charles, have I slept in the room with all that money? How could you place me in such danger? Your own mother!"

"As neither you nor any one else knew that the bags were there, mother, there is not much harm done. Besides, these people do not steal magnificently. A peon might take a silver dollar if he were a dishonest peon, just as a dishonest white man might; but the chances of escape are too few for a native to run the risk of stealing a large sum, even were he so minded. I knew there was nothing to fear, or I should never have put the bags behind your bed. Come now, mother; the trunks have gone, and we must follow."

As Winton divided the bags between two trusty men, he stood with Madam Winton for a few moments upon the veranda. Flandreau had not appeared, and was apparently oblivious of their departure. Totty's faint cough was heard inside.

"I veel drink de pink rum."

"*Point de rhum!*" It was Flandreau's voice, in tones decided though tender. There was a faint sob from Totty.

"I suffer so!"

"*Ça te tuera.*" The little anarchist's tone was like that of a patient mother to a persistent child.

The collection of small houses dignified by the name of town was silent as a sepulchre. The custom house, white with black-railed galleries high up on its sides, glittered clear in the tropical moonlight. The narrow way through which they passed between the houses was dark, but the broad plaza down by the water shone brilliant and clear in the bright night. The trunks and boxes had been put on board.

From the small row-boat which brought them alongside, Madam Winton stepped upon the deck of *La Madrugada*. Jones bowed low as he arose from his seat in the stern, and then reseated himself with his cigarillo.

"Well, well!" exclaimed Madam Winton, impatiently. "Start, man! Start!"

The two Spanish negroes looked inquiringly at Madam Winton.

Jones said, "Anchor no come," and relapsed, and whiffed.

"But it must come! Charles, tell him that it must come."

"He mus', but he won'."

"Come, come! Stir round, Jones. Why do you suppose Madam and I came down here in the middle of the night? To see you puff those wretched cigarillos? The shore breeze is rising! We must start! You know how soon the trades beat it down this time of year."

"Cian' git anchor. Cian' cut chain."

To these self-evident truths Madam Winton replied in one word, "Bosh!" And then, after a moment's reflection, "No wonder you've never been anybody."

As he took this to be a sweeping assertion covering the entire island, and not a personal remark, Jones puffed placidly.

"Have you all hauled together?"

"Yaas, Señor Don Carlos."

"Have you tried rigging a purchase with the throat halliards?"

"Try all t'ings," said Jones, who, be it frankly stated, had never heard of a throat halliard.

I

Winton, without more ado, unknotted the anchor rope from the painter; he then made a loop in the anchor rope, through which he thrust a long oar.

"Hoist your jib."

Jones looked lazily up at Señor Winton, who had ordered the Spanish negroes to haul on the jib halliards. There was a splash; the oar was floating as a buoy and guide to the whereabouts of the anchor, the sails were filling, and *La Madrugada* was pointing toward Caño Sandros, and gathering headway as she forged through the water. A mild surprise crept into Jones's seamed face; but second nature led him to the tiller, which he took in hand, pointed the bow for Santos Bay, and resumed his disturbed puffing.

"Go below, mother, and rest. Do!"

Madam Winton proved herself to be a sailor in appearance, if not in reality. She literally tumbled below. Señor Winton's black-and-tan, William Penn, had been their companion in all these moves. He also tumbled below. Madam Winton stretched herself upon the hard, low bench which was built into the side of the little cabin; but she got no more sleep that night. William Penn amused himself by tearing round her place of seclusion, now forward, now aft; scrambling under an old sail; rattling among oars and pieces of rope. First, he brought to light an immense beetle, in shape like a turtle, with legs raying out all round its circular shell. After he had made his first course off this delicacy, he sought for and found his dessert in the shape of a long centipede. Deftly he killed it, but before he had begun his second course, Madam Winton had tumbled up on deck again. She had not bargained for William Penn's idiosyncrasies.

When Madam Winton reached the deck, she found that they were moving along very smoothly, the water of the bay lap-lapping the sides of the boat.

Winton was stretched on a sail forward.

"Anything down there, Jones? Why can't Madam go down there?"

"Fo' de good Lawd, no! Don Carlos, de whole fo'ard pa't choked full ob centipedes."

"That's strange, Jones; a new boat, too!"

"Brought a load o' bananas ober to Señor Francoli, Don Carlos. Dis her fus' cruise, too."

"Bananas! Why, Andaluze is full of them! What is the mystery, Jones?"

"No myste'y, Don Carlos; on'y centipedes," declared Jones, stoutly.

Mrs. Winton gave a dignified scream, and sat down rather hastily upon the combing of the after hatch.

"Poor mother! What have you not gone through with, to come to me!"

The moon was now brilliant. By its light one of the Spanish negroes was spelling out in a six-months-old Spanish journal the Spanish news of the Cuban war. It was all victory for the Spaniards. This did not please the sailor over much, as the sympathies of the people of the islands were with the insurgents.

The boat glided along the tropical shore. There was a chill in the air now. Winton took up his travelling-rug, and wrapped it round his mother's shoulders. The high hills which they were passing were covered to the top with palm, iron-wood, and ceiba trees. Occasionally they passed a clearing where, set in the middle of a young banana field, a white house shone in the moonlight. Madam Winton watched the sluggish trail of the boat.

"What is that following us, Charles?"

Winton started, and looked backward. His mother's words brought up unpleasant memories.

"I see nothing, mother."

The boatman broke into the favorite song of "Sobre las olas."

"That is hardly appropriate now." Winton stood up, and gazed earnestly out over the water. "The waves have fallen, and so has the breeze, I fear."

"Don't listen to those wretched discords. There!" Madam Winton pointed. "Do you mean to tell me that you see nothing now?"

"Truly, I see nothing."

"I am not surprised; you are not looking where I point." Winton turned, and looked directly aft. He started slightly, but recovered himself on the moment.

"Some decayed log, probably, mother," he said reassuringly.

"Decayed logs do not follow boats. I am no child, Charles."

Winton did not dispute this self-evident fact; he said gently: —

"We shall leave it behind soon, mother. See! how the moonlight falls upon Señor Rizal's casa. Those girls are pretty, were educated abroad. They are fair — straight hair, but — but — "

"But?"

"Their brother is as black as night. No, no! such thoughts will never do. Yet they are — pretty. Where was Fanny Sands when you left, mother?" Then followed a talk of home, and dear home people, out upon the great tropical waste of waters — they two alone, at midnight. This thought came over Madam Winton. She looked apprehensively at the black boatmen and shuddered, drawing closer to Winton.

He gently drew the rug about her shoulders. His poor mother! He understood her, and she loved him. Just here, William Penn ran to the stern and barked furiously.

"Come here, sir!" ordered Winton.

William Penn slunk to his master's side.

"Lie down!" William Penn laid down.

After a while, not at all interested in Fanny Sands and her set, he stealthily crawled again to the stern. Jones, for reasons of his own, had, at that moment, reeled out his trolling line. A loop caught round one of William Penn's legs, and, in a moment, he was overboard. There was a shriek, almost human in sound, as the poor brute realized what his fate was to be. Winton sprang to his feet, and threw off his coat. Jones laid a strong hand upon him, holding his arm with iron grip.

"No, sah! See dah!" There was a quick rush; a long, black body turned over, its underside paling from white to delicate green through the medium of the water. A snap of cruel jaws — the sea was incarnadined. Winton staggered and put his hand over his eyes.

"My poor little dog!" he said, "my little dog!"

One of the Spanish negroes now came aft and whispered to Jones. There was a hurried consultation. Winton could not understand one word. The mixture of Spanish and negro dialect was far beyond his comprehension. He watched Jones anxiously. What could it mean? Jones arose, and handed the tiller to Winton.

"If de Señor be so keind," he said. He arose, and walked swiftly forward. Winton watched the three negroes as they disappeared through the forward hatch. Madam Winton sat gazing out wearily over the stern. She fancied that the black spot upon the water kept at a certain distance behind them.

"Lay your head upon my knee, mother," said Winton, soothingly. He said it more to keep her from looking forward, than for any other reason; he knew not what surprise might be in store for them. Then was heard the stumbling and scrambling of men's feet up the forward companion-way.

"Those boatmen seem anything but expert in climbing about, Charles. I wonder why you chose such stupid men."

"It's Jones's boat, mother. I had nothing to say in the matter. See how near we are running to the shore, mother; we cannot be far from our landing-place, now."

The stumbling and scrambling continued. The men seemed to be engaged in trying to raise some heavy weight to the level of the deck. Winton peered past the mast, and, watching thus, he saw them lift from the hatchway what seemed to be a human form. It lay limp and motionless. There was a pushing of the old mattress over the side. It and its burden parted company. A black face, which, even so, had a pallor of death upon it, floated past them. There was a second rush and snap behind the boat.

"What is all this mystery?" thundered Winton, as he dropped the tiller and started forward.

"Noah come heah!" warned Jones, in tones of horror, his hand raised to wave Winton back. "Noah come heah! Heah pooah native man. Come ovah almighty sick f'om de islands." Jones pointed seaward. "Him come in heah, I t'ink he on'y pain in hade. Him git wus. Him try git home to mudda in Haldez."

Winton turned white.

"Send one of those boys to the tiller."

Madam Winton had buried her face in her hands.

"Come here, Jones, to the mast."

They stepped aside. Winton glanced at his mother apprehensively. He spoke in low, fierce tones.

"Speak, man! He died of —"

"*Vomito negro,*" answered Jones. "It bad in Martinque."

"Good God! man, put us ashore."

Jones pointed to the high cliffs that now lined the near shore.

"No road, no shore.   Landin' jus' ahade." Jones shook his head mournfully.   "An' my new fin-keel ruin'."

FLANDREAU

FLANDREAU

FLANDREAU and Totty sat upon the veranda
of Flandreau's hotel at Andaluze. As usual,
Flandreau was carving pipes and talking anarchy. He spoke in French, Totty in the dialect of her mother, she being of that colony who
many years ago came from the slave states of
North America to settle on the shores of the
great tropic bay. The veranda was near the
rough path called a street; some young banana
trees made a pleasant shade in front of the little
whitewashed house.

"In the beautiful springtime we will leave
the islands, ma chérie, and will go north to the
home you never have see. In that splendid
city of the west I will again meet with my
brother conspirators, and we will plan against
the rich who do us poor so much injury."

Totty sighed. She had a pain in her breast,
and she did not care about anarchy. She gazed
at Flandreau with all the wonder that she could
command shining out of her sweet eyes. Her
eyes were different colors, one blue and the

other brown, and the very slight cast in them made them, Flandreau thought, adorable. Totty's feelings about Flandreau, though she could not put them into such words, were that he was a very contradictory sort of person. Flandreau, with his jovial smile, his wide mouth, his kind eyes, and his fierce talk of killing! Flandreau's tone was not fierce, — that, nature had prevented, — but his sentiments, learned from his society leaders, were terrible to hear.

"Has you eva keel any one?" It was almost too much effort for Totty to ask the question.

"No, mon enfant, but I go to begin now. I shall do what my society demands when I return to them. I am under their orders. We must be allowed to live." Flandreau flourished the knife with which he had just finished the beaded carving round the bowl of his pipe. "I shall slay two or three very rich men. That will make things more even."

How the even-ing process was to be accomplished Totty wondered, but she felt that it must be so. Flandreau said so, and Flandreau knew. Totty rose unsteadily upon her feet. She sighed and put her hand to her breast. She moved slowly into the little sitting-room, her slippers, which had grown so large of late, flap-flapping the boards of the floor.

" You like de gri'l' cakes fo' b'ekfas' ?" she asked and sighed.

" Whatever you provide, mon enfant, that is what I prefer."

Totty sighed as she walked with dragging step to the pantry; she sighed as she took down the old blue cup and measured it twice full of the precious white flour from the States; she sighed as she poured out the milk; and she sighed as she beat up the two eggs which Flandreau had found in a stolen nest that morning. She sighed again as she mixed the cakes and as she baked them, and as she put them on the plate, and as she brought them to the table. She sighed as Flandreau ate them, and he accompanied her sigh with a big one of his own to see that there were no more. It is wonderful that the cakes themselves, evolved amid such an atmosphere, did not sigh as they were being eaten. Then Totty dragged herself into her bedroom and solaced herself with a proud look at her white father's portrait. This portrait was an old-fashioned likeness of " Misser Thompson of Gainesville up No'th." Totty always went in and looked at this picture when she felt more sad than usual.

" Monsieur le Docteur goes to arrive to-morrow," said Flandreau.

Totty gasped and put her hand to her breast.

It was there that she felt the constant gnawing pain which was wearing her life away. She turned her head and gazed at Flandreau as an animal hunted to the death might look. The doctor coming! A sudden terror seized her. It was death if he did not come; death, perhaps, if he did. But no! Oh, no! Flandreau had said that she should live. The doctor could cure her, and he and she should walk as of old up the hill and watch for " Vapor Cleede " coming into the harbor, as Flandreau sat beside her and carved his pipes. And then, one day, when Flandreau had made enough money, they would sail away to that beautiful North, where Flandreau's society killed all the wicked rich.

Totty sat and rocked weakly in her chair, — the chair which Flandreau himself had made for her. Flandreau's great hound, Tzar, came and laid his big head in Totty's lap. It felt heavy, and Totty pushed it away, or tried to. Tzar would not go.

"Va t'en," said Flandreau. "Dost thou think that thou art wanted everywhere?" He pulled the great animal away, and made him lie at Totty's feet.

Then Flandreau went out to carry home some pipes that he had carved. He walked very fast. He hurried up the sloping, irregular street, with its low wooden houses upon either side. He hardly glanced at the verandas as he passed. He heard the tink-tinkle of the mandolin or guitar, and knew that the women were amusing themselves in the long hours while the men were at work, and they had nothing to do. They played "Sobre las olas," or "Para jardines Granada," and sang in their low, mellow voices. The odors were sweet; the thick, tropical foliage shaded the dusty road; but it was hot, and the way was long. Flandreau's legs were short, and he did not get over the ground very rapidly. When he arrived at the house of the banker for whom he had carved his handsomest pipe, he had hardly the breath to state his errand.

The banker's house was the most ambitious one in the little town. The banker himself was sitting on the veranda at the back of the house looking out over the bay. Flandreau was somewhat awed as he walked through the broad hall hung with pictures and furnished with furniture from France. The banker was sitting in an easy-chair under an awning of red and yellow. He was reading an old journal which contained accounts of the Cuban war. When he read of an insurgent victory, he said, Bueno! When he read of a Spanish victory, he shrugged his shoulders. He was smoking a long, black trabuco and drinking some very black coffee; but neither

K

the trabuco nor the coffee were quite so black as
the banker himself.

When he saw Flandreau appear hesitatingly
at the door of the hall which gave upon the
veranda, he smiled pleasantly, and welcomed
him in Spanish. Flandreau smiled his wide
smile, and shook his head. The banker vent-
ured on English, but Flandreau, having un-
limited faith in the banker's powers, replied in
French, which the banker drifted into without
effort or comment. Flandreau had heard that
the banker could speak ten languages; he believed now that it must be twenty. He spoke
French better than Flandreau himself, which
was not strange. Flandreau, in his wanderings,
had tried to pick up bits of other languages; and
as he was not an apt scholar, he had gained nothing in them, and had somewhat effaced his own.

The banker's wife came out on the veranda.
She was almost fair. Her hair was curly and
the color of bronze. Her features were rather
thick, but she was pleasant of face, and smiled
often. She wore a faded purple calico, which
seemed out of place with the mass of jewelry
which she carried in her ears and on her fingers.
She brought with her perfumes so strong as to
rival the odors of the flowers that crowned the
garden sloping to the sea. She passed behind
her husband and let her fingers rest on his shoul-

der for a moment with an intimate, caressing touch.

The Señora made Flandreau seat himself. She offered him coffee and dulces, which were still standing on the table from the late breakfast, and Flandreau took them, but was too much embarrassed to eat or drink. The banker admired his pipe, and paid Flandreau the price agreed upon, handing him also some trabucos. The banker's wife said something to her husband in Spanish.

"My wife asks how the Señora is to-day."

The Señora might mean anything; morals are easy at Andaluze. Flandreau's child-like mouth drew up pathetically.

"The doctor from Saltona goes to arrive to-morrow," he said.

The banker repeated his wife's second sentence: "Let us hope that it will come out well."

"Must it be done?" added the banker's wife, sympathetically.

When this was translated to Flandreau, he shook his head and said: —

"He says she will die without."

Then the Señora plucked a great bunch of allamanda blooms and flowers from the gorgeous Sangre de Cristi lily, and bracts from the bougainvillea vine, and gave them with many kind words, which he could not understand, to

Flandreau. And, at the Señora's orders, a Spanish servant brought a pot of guava jelly and a ripe pine, which Flandreau was asked to carry home.

When Flandreau laid the fruit and flowers in Totty's lap, she smiled faintly. When he told her what the banker and his wife had said, she looked up wonderingly.

"An' dose de reech you wan' to keel?"

"All rich are not like those, mon enfant."

"Does you know odder reech, F'and'eau?"

"It is true that I know no other rich, mon enfant, but that is not to say that other rich are not bad. Oh, yes; very, very bad, those rich!" Totty's sweet eyes looked toward the hill. She wanted so much to get up there, and see the bay again. There was a little cemetery on the hill, where a few poor headstones marked the last home of those from the North who had died in the unaccustomed climate.

"I like to get up to de g'ave-yaad, and look fo' Vapor Cleede," said Totty, between her sighs.

"Not to-day, mon enfant; Monsieur le docteur goes to arrive to-morrow. I will take you up there the day after to-morrow."

"You p'omise?" asked Totty, like a little child.

"I promise," answered Flandreau. Totty smiled. Flandreau always kept his promises.

"He will keep it," sighed Totty, with satisfaction, to herself. And she was not wrong; he did.

It would be so pleasant to be carried up the hill in Flandreau's strong arms; to lie there under the cabbage palm, and watch for the steamer once again, and when she got tired, to close her eyes and, as the soft sea-breeze caressed her cheek, to sleep. Oh! to sleep! When had she slept? Flandreau said that the doctor from Saltona would make her sleep.

"An' I shall sleep there, F'and'eau?"

"Yes, chérie, thou shalt sleep."

"I shall go the day after to-morrow," whispered Totty to herself.

The doctor arrived, — a surgeon unworthy of the name, who, having failed among the intelligent, had come to practise upon the ignorant. His orders were obeyed. Totty was made ready. Marietta, who swept out the custom-house office, came to be with her, and to aid the doctor. The unskilful knife began the deadly work; the unintelligent bandaging accomplished the rest.

When Totty was conscious, she whispered: —

"F'and'eau, shall we go to-morrow?"

"Not quite to-morrow; in a few days, ma chérie."

Totty looked up gratefully at the doctor; she had Flandreau's hard, red hand in hers.

"Don' talk any mo' o' killin', F'and'eau."

"I will only talk of what you bid me, chérie."

Totty's slim fingers stroked Flandreau's hand persuasively.

"I wou'n' keel dose po' reech, dey wan' to live, too, F'and'eau."

It was Flandreau who sighed now.   The fingers moved no more.

"I wou'n' keel dose po' reech, — it — is — so — nice — to — live."   And Totty died.

THE VALUE OF A BANANA LEAF

THE VALUE OF A BANANA LEAF

THE little Cristina was pushing the cacao car in and out of the drying-house. The car was not very heavy, for it was quite empty. The gathering season, which continues through several months, had passed, and all the ripe cacao had been cut, dried, and sold. The drying-house stood upon the estate of " Las Lilas."

After a time, Cristina got tired of her amusement. She pushed the car far back into the shed, and feeling somewhat weary with her utterly useless exertion, she lay down upon a bag which had been thrown upon some yagua. Lying behind the end of the car, upon the floor, she was quite screened from observation. She became drowsy, and would have slept, had she not been aroused by a rumbling sound. She knew the sound well. Some one was closing the doors of the drying-house. Was she to be imprisoned, then? Well, what matter? she could easily climb up to the eaves and call for help; some one must be passing, later; at present it was so cool, and so — hark! what was that? A step, and inside the drying-house! Ah! this, indeed, was of some interest! The little Cristina had always wished that something would happen; nothing ever happened down at the river patch where she lived, but surely, something was going to happen now! No one ever went into the drying-house and closed the door. On the outside, yes; but on the inside, never!

The little Cristina peered out from between the wheels of the car. The light was dim, but her eyes were young, and she recognized the intruder. It was 'Cito Mores. He had long been manager up at Las Lilas; now he was capitas, or foreman, since the Señora Sagasta had married Misser Williams, who had first come to her as manager.

'Cito Mores fastened the rolling door securely, and then he advanced into the drying-house, and, stepping upon the car over Cristina's head, he climbed up to the eaves, and from underneath the thatch of yagua, he took a bag. He got down, and laid the bag upon the platform of the car.

"'Cito Mores!" The voice came from the outside, near the drying-house. "'Cito Mores!" Dead silence. "Where can that rascal have gone?"

It was Misser Williams who called. Then the steps retreated; and 'Cito Mores was alone, so far as he knew. The little Cristina quaked. What if he should move the car! But it was no part of 'Cito Mores's plan to move the car. Its rumbling could be heard for some distance in the wood.

'Cito Mores sat quiet for a moment, and then, no longer hearing any stir outside, he opened the bag, and poured a stream of silver dollars out upon the car. Then Cristina heard the chink and clink of silver.

"He count the dollas," mused Cristina. "He leave the dollas; I take the dollas. Better far that I should have them than he. What did he ever do for me, this 'Cito Mores, — I, that bound up his leg when he fell through the bridge at Rojo Piedra? Did I get the thanks? No! Then shall I not take my thanks in his silver dollas? What then can I not buy? I will buy for the madre a fine pair of rings for the ears, like those of that grand Sibyl at 'El Monte.' I will buy for the little Tomacito a lovely machete belt; of red and green it shall be. For my father, — for my father, — nothing at all. Is it not he who always calls me the lazy one? Now we shall see who earns the most dollas, the father, or the lazy little Cristina."

Cristina lay there like a mouse, while 'Cito Mores counted up to two hundred and seventy-five. The dollars rolled and clinked upon the drying-car. The little Cristina would have liked to see them, they sounded so bright and shiny. A tap at the door, — "Tap-tap-tap-tap, tap-tap," — a signal, evidently. 'Cito Mores opened the door gently.

"Quiet, Francisco! He was here but now."

"All are there?"

"All."

"And when shall we bury them, 'Cito Mores?"

"This very night. The workmen come to-morrow to repair the yagua thatch."

"What do you think the safest place?"

Little Cristina's heart sank like lead. They would not leave them in the thatch, then; they were going to take them away!

"'Cito! 'Cito Mores!" It was Misser Williams's voice on the outside. "Where the devil is that rascal?" Again the steps retreated.

"Perhaps I had better call out and tell him," thought Cristina; "the dollas will never be mine, now."

"Rascal! And he can call the names! He! Rascal himself! He who takes all our little winnings from us; marrying that foolish woman who never counted her money, or knew how much she had. Listen to me, Francisco. You know the old palm tree down on the edge of the central grove, the one which the carpenter birds inhabit. Well, just below that there stands

a large mango tree.   It has been here for generations, they tell me."

"I know the old mango tree well, 'Cito Mores;
have known it all my life."

The little Cristina had also known the mango
tree all her life. Certainly, her life had not
been by many years so long as that of Francisco, but it had been quite long enough for her
purpose.

"Under those roots we must bury our treasure, Francisco; and then we must watch our
chance to get it away. To-night, at one o'clock,
we will come and take the bag. Come, now!
He may return for me."

'Cito Mores concealed the bag again among
the rustling yagua leaves, Francisco rolled the
door gently back, and they slipped out, leaving
the possessor of their secret behind.

The child was somewhat frightened at the
thought of what she intended to do, — for even
the Cristinas of this world have some sort of an
apology for a conscience, — but the joy of her
secret sustained her. Her thoughts absorbed
her so entirely, that her waking visions became
sleeping ones; she did not hear the men come
the second time, to remove the silver; and when
the workmen arrived in the morning, they were
surprised to see Felipe's little Cristina sit up
behind the drying-car, and rub her eyes.

"I baig of you not to tell mi madre," she said. "She think me with my grandmother. Felipe, he lick me well, if he know."

"The poor little Cristina!" they said, and promised.

On the morning after Cristina's night in the drying-house, she went to the central grove of which 'Cito Mores had spoken. After a slight search she found the place where 'Cito Mores and Francisco had buried the money. She clawed and dug with her little sharp nails all round the tree. Dried leaves had been carefully strewn; the artists had rivalled nature in their handiwork, and a stranger to their plans would have suspected nothing. Cristina, however, was one of the syndicate, and used her knowledge much as other members of other syndicates do at times. She looked out for number one. She intended at that time to be a silent partner, and, following in the footsteps of some silent partners, take all the proceeds.

When she tried to lift the bag, she found it very heavy; but she managed to drag it down to the bank of the river, which was not far away. The forest was deserted at that time; the men were all at their respective tasks, and she was not afraid of meeting any one until noontime. She knew of a fine place to deposit her gains. It was down the river below the ford, near the

Demarisi Casa. No one lived at the colonia now, and though the place was lonely, she should not go there at night, and there were no ghosts in the daytime. Her heart stood still when she thought of passing the night alone in the drying-shed. Thank the good God she had slept! If the ghosts had come they must have said, "That is Felipe's little girl; she is a very good child, —we will not waken her." Truly there must be good ghosts as well as bad ones!

Cristina searched about the bank of the river, which was now only a sluggish stream, and finally found the object of her quest. It was an old palm board which had been stranded along the shore; there were many such. The river was low; there was no danger in sailing upon it.

Cristina dragged her bag down to the shore, and seated herself astride upon the plank. She imitated a person walking, the board between her legs, her feet on the bottom of the river.

"That will be fine!" remarked Cristina.

She pushed her boat to the bank and tried to lift her bag on board. But as fast as she succeeded in getting the bag up on to the plank, it weighed the board down, and slipped off into the water.

"I must leave some of the dollas," said Cristina, sorrowfully.

Yesterday she would have thought one shining dollar a fortune; to-day two hundred and seventy-four were not enough within one dollar. However, needs must, as the old proverb hath it, and the devil was certainly driving Cristina very hard. She separated her hoard into two parts; about two-thirds she concealed in a hole in the bank. She sealed the entrance with a large stone, sprinkled some loose earth over it, drew a trailing behucca[1] across the place, gave a final admiring look at her handiwork, and started with the rest of her money for the secluded spot upon which she had settled. As she turned her head to look at her bank of safe deposit, she felt as much an artist in her way as 'Cito Mores and Francisco had been in theirs.

Luck watches over the helpless, and luck arranged it so that no one should see Cristina conceal her fortune.

"The good God will take care of it until I come again," said Cristina, piously.

Her voyage down the river was also successful. When she reached her second place of destination the sun was high. She heard the horn blowing from Brandon's colonia and from the banana plantation at Las Lilas.

"It is the rest hour," she said; "some one

---

[1] Bejuco, vine.

may come this way." She took her bag from
the boat and, like all the world before or since,
she pushed away with her foot the ladder of
salvation. The palm board floated down to
the sea, and its ungrateful passenger proceeded
to climb the river bank. She had but just
reached the top of the slope when she heard
voices; then she heard the rustle of footsteps
among the banana-trash. She flattened her
bag and fell quickly upon it; she closed her
eyes, and to all appearance slept the innocent
sleep of childhood. She heard the men pass
a little way from her and sit down on the bank
of the river beneath the shade of a mahogany
tree. They had brought their coarse food to
this spot to eat, and here to pass the hour of
noon. Luck again befriended the child: they
did not see her.

"Do you think Misser Williams has missed
it yet?" The voice was that of 'Cito Mores.

"Not yet, I think. It was a clever trick.
He said that no one but Francisco was to be
trusted."

The men chuckled over this. Cristina's ears
grew very large; she could fairly hear them
grow. Francisco continued:—

"What work of a moment when all had gone
to the festin at Haldez three days ago! He
so proud of his new wife, she so proud of her

new husband. She on the black horse, he on
the gray, the one that of old belonged to the
Señor Sagasta himself! Ay, ay, if he could but
see them now! What work of a moment it
was to quietly draw the nails out of the boards
at the back of the office. Did he think that we
are blind because we are peons? Did he think
that I had not sense to see that the back of the
desk stood close against the wall? The nails
out, how gently was the board laid upon the
ground! And then the sawing through the
desk! There was the difficulty, with that cat
the old Señora in the casa. Had she been
away, the work would have been done in a
quarter of the time. When the old Señora
called out, then indeed did I fear.

"'Francisco,' she said, 'do for the love of the
good God and all the blessed saints stop that
villanous noise. My poor head is splitting open,
and I would take my siesta. Dost thou think
that I remained at home to hear thy vile clamor?
Better far that I had gone to the festin! Oh,
for the days of the old Señor! then, indeed, had
I something to say.' And thou rememberest,
'Cito Mores, that the old Señor hated her as
the devil hates water from the Jordan."

"And then I came up," said 'Cito Mores,
"just in time to join you. A lucky dog am I
always."

"And told me to say, 'It will be over in a moment, Señora. It is a dog-house that Misser Williams wanted made to-day! I will take it round to the potrero presently.' And then for my lie I was forced to make a dog-house that very day. I lay that lie to you, 'Cito Mores."

"And why? One must lie only when it is necessary. I heard her order the dog-house myself. It is true. I did tell you to say it."

"Yes, it is true that she ordered the dog-house for his new hound. Nothing is good enough for Misser Williams now. But the old Señora! *She* loves him as the devil loves the lives of the saints."

"Ah! yes. It was dangerous, — sawing, — but that was necessary; else how should we have got through the back of the desk and swept out the lovely shining dollars; and I helped you replace the board, and sprinkle a little earth over the sawdust, and all was as before."

"You get but a quarter, 'Cito Mores; that was agreed upon."

"That we will see about later," said 'Cito Mores.

Cristina listened with horror to these revelations. She was lying upon some of that very silver. Silver stolen from Misser Williams up at Las Lilas. How wicked of them to steal from Misser Williams! Cristina's share in the matter seemed quite right to her. She was stealing from Francisco and 'Cito Mores. And who were they! And now she had by chance discovered that the money was not theirs, after all.

"What wicked men they are to steal from Misser Williams! So handsome a man!" The sex is the same the world over, and circumstances do so alter cases, that the chiefest of sinners abhors infinitesimal peccadilloes in others. "And they steal from Misser Williams!" whispered Cristina to a red and blue longicorn which crawled over her nose. "Thy feet shall go in the stocks, 'Cito Mores." Cristina remembered one happy day when Misser Williams had given her five centavos to spend at the bodega. That, however, did not prevent her hugging tightly the bag beneath her.

The noon hour ended, of which they were warned by the blowing of numerous horns; the pair arose to go. Cristina hoped that they would not discover her, but they strolled up the river bank and came upon the child.

"That girl of Felipe's, the brat!" said Francisco.

"The stocks for thee," said Cristina to herself.

"How she sleeps! Could she have heard, Francisco?"

"No! If I thought she had heard, I should pitch her into the river."

"Also the cep', Francisco." Cristina could think without moving her lips.

"Poor child! The sun is hot," said 'Cito Mores. He took his machete and cut a large paddle-shaped leaf from a wild banana. He thrust the end through some bushes that grew near the child, and bent the broad green blade above her head.

"Thou shalt not go into the stocks," resolved Cristina.

"Mercedes, her mother, is a devil," said 'Cito Mores.

"Thou shalt go in the stocks and the cep' also," whispered Cristina.

"The child is also bad; I would not trust her," said Francisco.   •

"For thee the cep', the stocks, and some lashes on the bare back," sentenced the listener.

"Not so bad," argued 'Cito Mores; "she bound up my leg when I fell through the bridge at Rojo Piedra."

"No prison, no lashes; the cep' for only one day," decided this vacillating judge.

"And when shall we take it from the mango glade, 'Cito Mores?"

"Not until the sailing of the next 'Vapor Cleede.' We will go, as other gentlemen have gone, perhaps to Turk's Island, and live like gentlemen."

"And if he discovers its loss?"

"He cannot discover its hiding-place."

Cristina hugged her bag the tighter.

"Thou art telling no lies for the first time in thy life, Francisco," she whispered.

"There goes the capitas; they are blowing the horn again, 'Cito Mores."

'Cito Mores did not stir. "Poor little thing," he said, "how tired she must be! I had a little girl once, Francisco, Clarita's child, but —"

"The pretty Clarita, who went off with —"

'Cito Mores turned a threatening look on Francisco. He drew his machete from his belt; Francisco turned and ran a few steps, but 'Cito Mores had long since ceased to take vengeance in behalf of Clarita; he used his machete only to cut several large leaves; with these he made for the child a perfect screen, and left her to her sleep.

The last words that Cristina heard from 'Cito Mores were, "She is a good little thing," from Francisco, "Let her bake!"

As the men struck into the path which took them back to their work, Cristina pushed away her covering, and sitting up looked after them.

She shook her fist in rage at Francisco's tattered back.

"The cep', the stocks, the lash, the platoon of soldiers. Death! death! death! thou devil Francisco, and that is far too good for such as thee. And for 'Cito Mores no prison, no cep', no lashes, and perhaps, who knows, if he is very kind, one of my silver dollas. But alas! then I shall have but two hundred and seventy-four. Perhaps he will want no money at all, but I shall always be kind to thee, 'Cito Mores, and when I buy a great banana walk, with my fortune, and have servants to wait on me, who knows but I will let thee have a place on my plantation; but my silver chest will always stand in the middle of the room, 'Cito Mores. That shall be when I am grand Señora, and Francisco is hanged."

It was not a matter of much time to hide the bag under the root that she knew of, which overhung the bank; and then, thoroughly rested, she returned to the canucca[1] of her father, Felipe. Arrived at home, she found the family in so great a state of excitement that they listened but little when she informed them that she had been since yesterday with her grandmother.

Misser Williams had been robbed. He had just discovered his loss. It must have occurred some

---

[1] Small patch of land, probably a corruption of *caducar.*

days ago. Three days since, he had gone with the Señora to the festival at Haldez. Every one from the plantation had gone but the old Señora and Francisco. The doors were all locked, no one could have entered, and, when Misser Williams returned, he found his desk locked as he had left it. To-day, when he had searched, the traces of sawdust and other evidences of thievery showed plainly how the money had been taken ; but who was the thief ? Ah ! that was the mystery. This very day he had gone to his desk to get some money, had opened it with his key, and lo ! the money was not there.

" Thy poor, hard-working father goes to him, this Don Jack-Tom ; he claims his four dollars the terrea.[1] He had been cleaning for an entire week past, save only the blessed Sunday when we all attended the cock-fight, the festival day, the day when he went to Haldez after the new bull, and one other day when the rum got into his legs. On those days, naturally, he could not clean, and yet, when he goes to demand his week's wages and a trifle in advance, what does he hear ? ' Felipe, you have cleaned only three days since I paid you last. I will give you what you have earned, but I will not pay you in advance.' Ay, ay, for the good old times when

---

[1] A measure of land.

the Señora never knew if she had paid, or if one had worked. And then that wicked one goes to the desk, opens it, and lo! the money is gone! and thou away with thy grandmother a night and day, and no one to care for the little Tomacito, and see that he gets not the banana belly."

The little Tomacito's profile as to figure was proof positive that there had not been an ounce of prevention, and, as his clothing consisted of a crownless straw hat, the result of his gorging was most apparent. He sat upon a log in front of the cabin, alternately eating his banana, and shouting *"Libertad! Libertad! Libertad!"* as fast as he could articulate, and, unlike most reformers, he practised what he preached.

" I buy for the muchachito a machete with my earnings."

" Thy earnings?"

" I work hard when I go away." Cristina was at times truthful. She measured with an appreciative eye the rotund form of the little Tomacito. She might find a belt that would compass the circle, but she sighed as she saw herself trying to keep the belt in place. But Tomacito must have a belt and machete like other boys. That was certain. Felipe claimed to have been a warrior at four years of age. Tomacito must be one at three.

Then Cristina began to haunt the forest. Sometimes she left the cabaña in the morning, and was gone for hours. At these times, she returned with her little paws very muddy. She said that she had been searching for roots, and brought home a few withered ones, from time to time, to avert suspicion. During these absences, she visited both hiding-places, and counted her money as a miser does his hoard. She chuckled inwardly as she saw the gradual gloom that was settling over Francisco. 'Cito Mores looked anxious also; he and Francisco searched furtively the faces of all with whom they came in contact; but they never thought of looking into the face of the little Cristina.

Then Cristina took to staying away a day or two at a time. She was at her grandmother's, she told them at home. Her peace-offering, on the first day of her return, was a belt for Tomacito; a belt of red and green squares, and, thrust through the holder, was a cheap, little machete. She buckled the belt round Tomacito's rotundity; its only fault lay in the fact that it would slip up or down. Then she put upon his head Felipe's best Panama hat, the one that he always wore to the cock-fight, and sent him forth to fight imaginary foes.

"*Libertad! Libertad! Libertad!*" squeaked the little Tomacito, in his child's treble.

"You must kill thieves; those who steal, muchachito," said Cristina, with great earnestness; "nothing so bad as thief."

"*Libertad! Libertad! Libertad!*"

After Cristina's second return she produced a pair of large gold hoops; these she clasped with pride in her mother's ears.

"And to buy them? They must cost money!" Mercedes did not wish to be too inquisitive; it might involve the loss of the ear-rings.

"Indeed, madre mia, I must work hard to gain all that."

"Padre Martinez has sold them to her," inwardly reasoned Mercedes; "that makes it right."

Sometimes Cristina's hands were very clean, sometimes they were very dirty. Cristina had never heard it said that cleanliness is next to godliness. If that saying were true, then Cristina could never hope to be clean. But when Cristina chose to remove the dirt stains she was successful. Whatever she did she did thoroughly, and there was the whole river back of her.

A month had passed since Cristina had spent the night in the drying-shed. One day she had gone up to Las Lilas on an errand for her mother about soap for the washing, and while there the old Señora had set her to work mending her hammock. There were no drones in the old Señora's hive, always excepting the young Señora.

The young Señora was sitting in her hammock, holding one of those dress rehearsals for which she was famous. The scarlet pillow was at her back, the scarlet shawl trailed upon the floor, she wore a pale blue gown now, and a pretty falling ruffle round her neck. Misser Williams's step was heard; she fastened the rose a trifle more securely over her ear, she pulled the comb a little higher, and the black curl a little lower, and was ready for the renewed conquest that she made every time that his eyes rested upon her. Misser Williams came up the broad veranda steps.

"I am afraid that we shall have to go without the long chain and the gold lorgnon, my Rose," he said; "the money that I was saving for your birthday present is quite gone."

The Señora pouted.

"But I have plenty, have I not, Misser Williams. Cannot I buy it for myself?"

"If you will, my Sweet! if you will! but I had hoped to give to you."

"All is yours that is mine, Misser Williams," she said.

"No! no! that is not the same. The other was mine; I had fairly earned it as your manager, Suzon. It will be some time before I can save up so much more."

"That is because my manager spends every-thing on the plantation. Let us begin now and spend a little on ourselves."

Misser Williams shook his head. He took the pretty dark fingers of the Señora in his.

"The husband must be as faithful to his trust as the manager," he said. "When we are once more upon our feet we will have a half-dozen lorgnons and a dozen gold chains; now — "

He finished the sentence by kissing the Señora's finger-tips. Cristina saw the sad look in Misser Williams's gray eyes.

"Even when I am grand Señora I shall never have a gentleman like Misser Williams to love me," she thought.

Misser Williams looked up and for the first time caught sight of the little Cristina. He colored like a boy. Misser Williams's tender moods were not on exhibition.

"How long has that child been here?"

"All the morning; she came with a message, and mamma kept her to mend her hammock, of which, however, I suppose she knows nothing."

"The loss of the money does not trouble me so much as the thought that we have thieves among us."

Cristina gazed intently at Misser Williams as he said these words.

"I have trusted them all; I have thought them all faithful."

Cristina could bear the sad look in the kind gray eyes no longer. "He has trusted us all," she repeated to herself. "It is true. That he has." She made a sudden resolve. She would tell Misser Williams all. She looked at the little clock which hung above the Señora's head. She could not tell time,—there were a few things that the little Cristina did not know, and this was one of them, — but she could watch the second hand, and when it flew round to the little mark at the top she would begin to tell. Cristina was somewhat in the frame of mind of the traditional drowning man, whose entire life passes in review in the twinkling of an eye. Her past rushed pell-mell before her eyes, and her dreams of the future clamored for notice also.

"If I tell, I can never buy a banana walk, and be grand Señora; and Francisco and 'Cito Mores and me, we will sit in the stocks for some days, perhaps; perhaps they will keep us in the cep' for a year; perhaps they will take us to Saltona and shoot us dead. But Misser Williams, his looks are kind; he did give me those five centavos; he shall have his pesos." She advanced slowly toward Misser Williams. She glanced at the second hand. It was nearly round the circle. She would be a rich girl for a few seconds more.

"And I offered a very fair reward, it seems to me."

Ah! here was a hope. Perhaps she would not be shot, after all. She turned her head toward the clock. The hand was three seconds past the point she had decided upon.

"How much you give, Misser Williams?"

"How much do I give? For what? What's the child talking about? For your mending the hammock? That is the Señora Cordeza's. I do not keep the Señora Cordeza's accounts."

The mother-in-law problem was no nearer solution at Las Lilas than anywhere else on the habitable globe.

"I am upon other subjects than hammocks; much more serious ones, Señor. How much do you offer to him who finds your dollas?"

"Who finds my dollars, child? Don't be stupid."

"You will find much else in me beside the stupidity, Señor. What is the price you offer?"

Misser Williams sighed. "They are gone, past recall," he said.

Cristina persisted, annoyingly. "How much, Señor?"

"I offered twenty dollars reward, Cristina. But of what use to talk of it? The money is

gone." Misser Williams slipped the plain gold
hoop up and down on the Señora's finger.

"Must anything be disclosed?"

"Disclosed? What curious English the child
speaks! Disclosed?"

"Must one tell the whole truth?"

"No! 'No questions asked,' as we say in
the States. I believe the child knows something, Suzon. But how could you, of all persons on the plantation, know anything of my
money, Cristina?"

Cristina held out her hand.

"The twenty dollas," she said.

The manager rose.

"What can she mean, Misser Williams?"

"And you would steal my money! you! the
little Cristina?"

Cristina could not bear the tone of Misser
Williams's voice.

"I did not steal it from you! I did not
steal it from you, Señor!" she almost shouted.
"Give me twenty-one dollas, — bright, silver
dollas, — and I will take you to where the
money is."

Cristina's sudden accession of tender feeling
did not prevent her from driving a sharp bargain.

Misser Williams could not believe his ears.
He entered the office, and from a well-mended

desk, standing in the middle of the room, he took twenty-one glittering Mexican dollars. Cristina looked them carefully over, and rejected three which seemed to her scrutinizing eye to have lost something of their first freshness, and another, which was somewhat battered upon the edge. When the Señor had allowed her to choose four others in place of them, she walked down the veranda steps.

"Come," she said.

"Where?" asked the dazed manager.

"Where the devil has been before us," answered Cristina.

The Señora arose from the hammock.

"I would go also, Misser Williams, but the woods are damp, and my slippers are thin—" She began the usual dress rehearsal by lifting, ever so slightly, the hem of her gown; but, for the first time since she had known Misser Williams, his ears were deaf, his eyes were sightless. In Cristina she had found her rival.

The child led the young American to the first hiding-place, under the mango tree. She described how the devil had taken the money, and had hidden it there. Then they walked rapidly to the river bank; and in the second hiding-place, when the stone was removed, did Misser Williams find two-thirds of the lost money. The little Cristina then made the manager follow

M

her down the stream and across the ford, to the place where she had slept, a month ago; and there she dug from under the roots, of which Cristina alone knew the secret, the remainder of the stolen property. She counted out the money. There were nine dollars missing.

"I have had to spend some trifling sums," said Cristina. "Nine of your dollas I have taken; but I will at once pay you back. I am one who always pays my debts."

From the twenty-one dollars which Misser Williams had paid Cristina as her reward, she counted out nine of the dullest into his outstretched palm, her manner as grand as if she were still going to be the Señora she had hoped, and as if at that moment her bank account had not ceased to exist.

"I am now possessed of twelve dollars," said Cristina. "It is not a fortune, but, with economy, it is enough. I shall buy Tomacito a spur with which to ride the bull, when he is of age, to carry the suckers for the Señor; I shall buy la madre a ring like the Señora's," — Misser Williams had paid one hundred dollars for the diamond at the city; "I shall keep the rest to educate Tomacito."

"And your father?" Misser Williams was smiling broadly.

"Nothing will Felipe get. That will please me best, Señor."

"And you will educate Tomacito where?"

"At our own canucca, Señor. I raise a fine young cock for the muchachito. When the good God allows him to become a little smaller round, he will make a very good cock-fighter,—as good as the Padre Martinez, perhaps even better."

This rose-tinted view of the future of the little Tomacito was broken in upon rudely by Misser Williams.

"And the thieves?"

"Your compact says *that* I need not reveal, Señor. But of one I joy in telling, and that one is the Francisco. It was the Francisco who sawed the boards. It was the Francisco that took the money. It was the Francisco that hid it under the yagua thatch, and again under the mango tree. It was the Francisco who said 'Let her bake!' It was the Francisco who said, 'The child is bad, I would not trust her.' Put the Francisco in the stocks; put the Francisco in the cep'; give the Francisco lashes on the bare back; hang the Francisco if you will, Señor, but the other I will not name. No; not if you take me to the town and let the soldiers *shoot me dead!* " —which shows the value of a banana leaf.

When Misser Williams arrived at the casa of

Las Lilas, the Señora had just finished a very satisfactory dress rehearsal.

When Cristina arrived at her father's canucca with her twelve dollars, the little Tomacito was in his usual costume. Brandishing wildly the small machete, he shouted, *"Libertad! Libertad! Libertad!"*

ANASTASIO'S REVENGE

DON BILLY BLAKE was gowned in a costume of pale green. It was stiffly starched, and the coat stood out like a woman's jacket. The trousers were very wide, and were creased on the sides instead of in the front, so that on the inner side the legs fought for precedence. They sounded flip-flap, flip-flap, at each two steps of the Señor Don Billy, and the cause for that sound must have rendered locomotion painful.

Don Billy had come over to Las Palmas to complain. The English capitas, whom he had engaged, had suddenly left his employ, and had taken a contract to build a road for Señor Winton. Consequently, Don Billy was wroth.

Winton had been planting cacao all the morning. He wore some ragged pajamas, and a pair of slippers very much down at the heel. Cacao planting requires much close contact with Mother Earth, both for the man who makes the small hole in the ground by the already driven stake, and for the man who follows with the pail of seed in its paste of wood ashes, and pulverizes

167

the rich earth over the black germ, and leaves it to its Creator.

"You got 'Nastasie, too," said Don Billy, when he had finished his plaint.

"I did not engage Anastasio, Don Billy."

"But he's here," argued Don Billy.

"But he can't be here."

"But he is here."

"Well, then, Brown must have engaged him. I know nothing about it. I contract with Brown, and he engages the men; I have nothing to do with the men. My business is all with Brown, my English capitas."

"Your English capitas! Sounds mighty fine. He was my English capitas until I kicked him off the finca."

"Then I don't see what you're growling about," said Winton, good-naturedly.

"Well, I wanted my drain built."

"But if you kicked him off — "

"Look out for him, that's all."

Don Billy flip-flapped along the veranda like an enormous katydid, and climbed with some difficulty into one of the swinging chairs which stood ready for venturesome visitors by day, and creaked in the wind the long night through.

"I heard from Juan that Anastasio had left you in the press of your work, Mr. Blake." Madam Winton had joined the group. "I had my say to Anastasio, although I do not speak his mongrel tongue. I expressed my opinion through Alphonse and Juan; for justice is justice, Mr. Blake, and right is right."

Don Billy flapped his legs; they seemed to say, "Hear! hear!"

"All signs fail down here, mother. Justice is perverted, and right is generally wrong. How did you communicate with Anastasio? Of course I know you'd find a way." Winton had unbounded faith in his mother's powers.

"You see, Charles, Anastasio speaks a mongrel sort of Spanish. Dupré speaks it too, as well as French. Alphonse can speak a little French, but no Spanish. So I had to tell Alphonse to tell Dupré to tell Anastasio what I thought."

"What did you think, mother?"

Madam Winton put on her most severe expression.

"I told him that he could not serve God and Mammon."

Winton cast a glance downward at his heelless slipper and frayed coat sleeve, and then raised his eyes to where Don Billy sat, green and starched, in the swinging chair.

"I don't think that I look at all like Mammon, mother, and I am sure that Don Billy doesn't look very much like — "

"Charles! Don't be irreverent."

"Like Mammon, mother," Winton ended, lamely. "What do you pay a day, Don Billy?"

"I pay one-fifty Mex. per day; won't pay no more."

Nothing could have prevented Don Billy's "per." He considered that the word necessarily belonged to a business conversation.

"Ah! You see Brown has promised them one-seventy-five."

Don Billy's thoughts did not appear with great regularity. There were deep chasms of blanks between the spots that might be said to indicate thought. This was quite satisfactory, for when Don Billy really did put his mind to it he could think to some purpose. He hated to have to think, it was so much trouble; and other people hated to have him.

"Niggas is niggas!" said Don Billy; "but you do expect some decent treatment from a white man."

"Am I white, Don Billy?"

"Whitest man round yere," answered Don Billy, in good faith, not noticing Winton's amused smile. "Brown's *skin's* white."

"I do not like this constant association with these negroes," said Madam Winton, whose family had been of a distinct abolition stripe. "I must say that I do not care at all for the company that I am forced to associate with."

"Mother, if you can't have what you like, wouldn't it be better to try to like what you have?" urged Winton.

"That is very hard work, Charles. Don't let those Williamses come over here; I do not like that woman at all."

"I thought that hostilities had ceased. Don Billy, the front slope down there is full of buried hatchets, and now my mother wants me to dig one up and hurl it through the air at Williams, over at Las Lilas."

"No; he is well enough."

"All the women adore him, and I find that my mother is not behind the —"

"She is so vain. Such a peacock! she prims and plumes —"

"She *is* a peacock, mother, but she has nothing vicious about her. Oh! how do you do, Williams? buenos dias, Señora! — Mother, the enemy is upon us! Do be nice to them, for my sake."

Misser Williams and the Señora from Las Lilas had just appeared over the crest of the hill. She was riding a white bull, which looked gayly in its red trappings. Williams was seated on the gray which had belonged to Señor Sagasta, the Señora's first venture. Madam Winton walked to the edge of the veranda, shaded her eyes with her hand, and gave the Señora a stiff bow, into which she tried to infuse a modicum of graciousness. The Señora saw her lips move.

"I wonder what that severe lady is saying of us, Misser Williams."

"She is saying 'How beautiful the Señora is looking this morning!' my Rose."

The bride simpered, and pulled her curl a little lower. What Madam Winton was really saying, was : —

"Oh, dear! Charles, don't you think the table-cloth we had at dinner, last night, will do ?"

"Economy is filth," returned Winton, sententiously.

"You should write a book of proverbs." Madam Winton smiled. She did sometimes. Her son's imperturbable good nature was irresistible. With such a nature as his, one becomes utterly exasperated, or utterly hopeless. The latter mood is best; by it, contention is discouraged.

The Williamses were at the back steps.

"Oh! come round to the front," called Winton; "we don't expect the ladies to dismount there, Williams."

The great white bull was led round to the front steps, and Winton ran down to meet them; but he was not quick enough, for Misser Will-

iams had dismounted, and thrown the bridle to
his ragged little groom, and taking the Señora
in his strong arms had lifted her down, and set
her upon the steps.

"And how is the Queen of Sheba?" asked
Winton, gallantly; the while Madam Winton
groaned in Don Billy's ear: —

"Will you look at our neat front path, all cut
up by that great bull's hoofs. I wish that you
could have heard Charles scolding Pedrito for
it this very — oh! how do you do, Señora? How
do you do, Mr. Williams? And," she added, at
a look from Winton, "you have come to breakfast, of course."

The Señora primmed and plumed, and finally,
with many little screams and pretences of fear,
and with the aid of Winton and her husband,
climbed up into the second swinging-chair. Don
Billy tried to extricate himself from his height
to assist at a function which appeared to be so
delightful; but he had only partly freed himself,
when he saw that the Señora was seated. He
leaned back with a sigh.

Madam Winton looked on at the Señora's
antics with a severely disapproving mien. She
considered that the protrusion of the little slipper, so far beyond the short, flounced skirt,
verged too closely upon the borders of immo-
rality. The Señora's costume seemed very the-

atrical in Madam Winton's eyes. Her scarlet
shawl was trailing upon the floor, a red rose
nestled behind her small ear, a mantilla of
black lace fell in a point over the high tor-
toise-shell comb, and the curl in front of her
forehead seemed darker and more drooping
than ever. She had demanded the attention
of Winton and her husband for fully five minutes, and got herself settled only after many
little shrieks and timid cries.

Madam Winton was one of those mothers
who dislike to see her son "made a fool of,"
as she would express it. Winton was one of
those men who delight in everything that is
pretty and charming, no matter how false he
knows it to be; and he frankly expressed his
mind when he said that he "loved to be made
a fool of."

The Señora's foil, Don Billy, swung fatly in
the opposite chair. A naturalist, seeing them
from a distance, would have swooped down upon
the veranda at Las Palmas, as containing two
new varieties of the mammoth insect tribe, —
one curious and one brilliant, — which had not
heretofore met his eye.

"You will remain for breakfast and dinner," said Winton, recklessly regardless of the
daggers in Madam Winton's eye, the law of
hospitality, in that most hospitable country,

taking precedence, even over Madam Winton's wishes.

"Two clean table-cloths!" groaned Madam Winton, in Alphonse's sympathizing ear.

Winton suddenly became conscious of the down-at-heel slippers and the ragged pajamas, and disappeared hurriedly, to appear later as the spotless colono that his guests had always known him.

Madam Winton wanted to ask, "To what are we indebted for the honor of this visit?" Her curiosity was soon set at rest by Misser Williams.

"Do you happen to know where Brown, the English capitas, is working now, Winton?"

"Here; for me."

"He promised to come to me yesterday, and I have paid him in advance for clearing my potrero."

"Same case here," growled Don Billy.

"Your English capitas, of whom you are so proud, seems an unreliable creature, Charles."

"So he does, mother, but he has the faculty of making the peons work."

Madam Winton disappeared for a moment, to suggest to Alphonse two extra dishes.

"You'll have trouble with him," gurgled Don Billy.

"I don't care, so that he does my road."

"Where are they working now, Don Billy?"

"On the other side of the trocha. 'Nastasie took off his hat and bowed to me just as if he hadn't left me to go with Brown."

"It is custom that makes cowards of us all," said Winton.

"Don't you mean conscience?" Madam Winton had no sense of humor.

"I never thought that my conscience was custom-made, mother."

Don Billy had been sitting, thinking, for fully two minutes. Rather, he had successfully passed over a blank space, and arrived at an oasis where thought triumphed over vacuity.

"'Nastasie, too! I thought that fellow would feel a little gratitude."

"He looks for gratitude! and is free, white, and twenty-one!"

"Charles, don't interrupt Mr. Blake. Why, Mr. Blake?"

"Well, he came to me away along back and asked me to send to the States for three things for him. And I sent. I suppose he'll get 'em; they're things that a custom-house officer wouldn't want."

"Is there anything that a custom-house officer cannot make useful?" asked Winton, laughing.

"Well, you can judge. They were a map of the world—"

"No! Too well satisfied with their own little island!"

"A Bible and a toothbrush."

"For the last two named the native has no possible use; they ought to come through in perfect safety, Don Billy."

"He didn't give me no money," argued Don Billy; "and I haven't got any use for the things when they do come."

"Beffus," said Alphonse.

When the visitors had been safely assisted from their gibbets and were seated at the table, —

"Did you give San José any money?" asked Misser Williams.

"San José?" Winton looked bewildered.

"The men always call Brown 'San José,'" said Don Billy. "He came from there. Have you advanced him any money, Winton?"

Winton looked uneasily at his mother, and hesitated.

"A — a little," he said.

"How much, Charles?"

"About forty dollars."

"Rather you than me," said Don Billy, with more force than grammar.

"Charles Winton!"

"It was my money, mother," said Winton, meekly. "Why, Don Billy, isn't he honest?"

"Look out you get the work done, that's all."

N

Cigarettes, coffee, and liqueurs agreeably accompanied the next half hour. The afternoon passed delightfully to all but Madam Winton: as the Señora climbed again to the swinging-chair and tinkled upon the mandolin and sang some pretty songs. "Sobre las olas" was asked for several times, even Don Billy joining in the chorus. The afternoon ended at last, as all afternoons pleasant or disagreeable must do. Madam Winton saw, with a grateful sigh, that her guests were preparing to depart. Winton was vehement in his invitation to the Williamses to remain. Madam Winton's politeness increased as she saw that they had determined upon saying farewell. The white bull was brought round again to the front steps. Misser Williams lifted the Señora in his arms like a little child, and seated her upon the aparejo. There was the usual demonstration. The Señora made an apparently earnest though futile attempt to cover the black slipper with the flounce of her skirt; but it would show, and a large bit of the open-worked white stocking with it. When the Señora was seated, Misser Williams handed her the scarlet shawl, Winton adjusted the gay saddle-cloth, and Don Billy fatly puffed and blew in trying to ascertain if the aparejo straps were securely fastened. The Señora, having all the men about her, was supremely happy, and pulled the black curl lower and flattened it upon her forehead, looking archly at Winton the while from liquid eyes. She drew the rose forward, she raised the comb a trifle, and threw the mantilla again gracefully over it, opened her fan and waved it as only one of her race can do, and disappeared over the brow of the hill, a vision of beauty. When Don Billy Blake could see her no more, he called for his steed.

"Pretty nice thing to fall heir to old Sagasty's horses as well as his wife," growled Don Billy.

The roan was brought, and Don Billy mounted from the veranda. Once in the saddle, he was master. "No one can't touch Don Billy on horseback," Perkins of Haldez had said, and when one discovered what idea Perkins meant to convey, one agreed with him. Don Billy did not start at once; he knew that he wanted to say something. The chasm was nearly past, the oasis was in sight.

"Oh! Yes, that was it. Look out Brown don't fool you."

"He said that he wanted to pay the men," said Winton, sheepishly.

"Better give 'em vales [1] on the bodega." Don Billy stuck desperately to his oasis. "That ain't

[1] Orders.

your business either; I suppose Brown takes the contract. Well, so long! rather you than me." Don Billy looked down at his coat. "I'd rather be green outside than in." With this parting shot, he nodded to Winton, removed his enormous Panama in response to Madam Winton's stiff bow, and clattered down the slope.

The following day saw Winton on his way to Caño Sandros to see the company's agent about some furniture which he expected from the North. He returned just as the sun was setting. When Winton dismounted, Anastasio was seated upon a tree trunk by the back steps.

"Is that you, Anastasio? buenos dias!"

Anastasio arose respectfully.

"Buen' dia', Señor; I should like to have a short conversation with the Señor when he has eaten."

"Certainly, Anastasio. Come to me after dinner."

When Winton, being refreshed with bath and dinner, sat sipping his coffee, he heard a slight tapping on the floor of the veranda at his feet. He looked down and saw Anastasio. The veranda at that corner stood six feet from the ground; Anastasio's head came five inches above the floor, — that is, the top of it. He was a powerfully built man of the Spanish-negro type. His face was black and shining, and his features handsome. Winton noticed his splendid teeth as he

opened his mouth to speak. Anastasio had removed his hat.

"May I speak with the Señor?"

"Oh, it's you, Anastasio; I had forgotten you.
Well, what is it?"

"I think that San José has gone, Señor."

"San José? Oh, you mean Brown. Gone?
Gone where?"

"We know not, Señor; we think he has gone
to 'The City.'"

"Why should he go?"

"I know not, Señor. He said, the night before
last, the night before the day that Misser Williams came over with the Señora, that the
Señor had relieved him of his work."

"I have not seen him," said Winton.

"He started, I think, the night before Misser
Williams was here. He said that the Señor
would finish the work himself, and that we were
to look to the Señor for our payment. I have
to get my money, Señor."

"The scoundrel! Did he tell you that? I
have no contract with you, Anastasio. How
much does he owe you?"

"Thirteen dollars, Mexican, Señor. He owes
all the men for their work."

Winton thought, with a sigh, of his forty dollars, and his trust in the word of the English
capitas. He began to feel extremely foolish.

Don Billy's words came back to him. Anastasio stood looking at him expectantly.

" I made no contract with you, Anastasio. He was to engage the men and pay them himself. I have no agreement with you; you know that."

" And am I to have no payment for my hard work, Señor?" Anastasio argued with the persistency of the islander, nothing being accomplished without much time spent in this, to him, agreeable pastime.

" You have no claim on me, Anastasio. How do you think that I feel? I have advanced Brown forty dollars, besides what I had already paid him for work done."

" But how am I to be paid, now that San José has departed, Señor?"

" Do you mean to say that he has paid you nothing?"

" Not a centavo, Señor."

" How could you be so foolish?"

Anastasio grinned broadly.

" I have not advanced him money, Señor, and unlike the Señor I should not have advanced it if I had had it."

Madam Winton had not spoken thus far. She now asked an explanation. Winton gave it to her, not without some mortification on his part.

" I told you so, Charles." She always did, before and after.

"So you did, mother."

"So did Mr. Blake. Why can't you listen to your elders?"

"Did anybody, ever?"

Anastasio bowed to Madam Winton; he then replaced his hat, took from his many-colored belt two machetes, and walked up the slope, alongside the veranda, and round the casa. Then Winton heard the sharpening of the blades upon the grindstone. The burrr, burrr, buzzz, buzzzzz, made an unpleasant accompaniment to his own unpleasant thoughts. Forty dollars Mexican was not, to be sure, very much money, but he was trying to see how economically he could run the plantation for the year; and then, too, he felt a great diminution of respect for his own intuitive powers as regarded character. Brown had seemed so open and so pleasant. To be sure, Don Billy and others had complained of his breaches of contract. These complaints had amused him. It is one thing to listen to your neighbor's woes, and another thing when they come home to you. Winton heard the footsteps of a horse, and had hardly turned when Don Billy shouted, as he came dashing up the hill: —

"I told you so!"

"I know you did," said Winton. "There is a pair of you."

Don Billy had started on his hasty errand in just the clothes that he had on. His home toilet would hardly have been the proper one for an afternoon tea. · His costume consisted of an old pair of trousers, very ragged and much stained with the juice of the green banana, so that Don Billy appeared like a murderer fleeing from justice. He wore a cotton shirt which had once been red. Large lozenges of lilac made this garment utterly hideous.

When Winton said, "There is a pair of you," Madam Winton exclaimed, "Don't be disrespectful, Charles." She could not quite bear such implied intimate companionship with the spotted bearer of reproach.

"I told you so! I said, give 'em vales on the bodega, didn't I, now? and they — tell — me that you gone and give' that rascal forty good dollars."

"I told you so, myself. I shouldn't give him forty bad dollars, I shouldn't know where to get them; besides, there's a prejudice against giving even rascals bad dollars. The money was my own. Did you think that I had given Brown your money?"

"N-n-no," answered Don Billy. The usually meek worm had turned.

Burrr-burrr-buzzzz-buzzzzz, went the grindstone. Don Billy peered round the corner at Anastasio.

"So you got left?"

Anastasio answered in his mongrel Spanish : —

"I am not left so badly as I will leave San José, Señor."

"What are you sharpening machetes for at this late hour of the evening?" inquired Winton, not without some misgivings.

"Kill San José."

"Where's he gone?" asked Don Billy.

"City."

"How do you know?"

"I think it must be so.   Tre' Pelo' met him far up beyond the cattle farm the night before last."

"You can't catch him now."

"Catch him on the vega."

"Charles! are you going to allow this cold-blooded murder?"

"I thought you were anxious about those forty dollars, mother."

Winton having recovered his good humor could not forbear a little teasing, considering what had gone before.

"Forty dollars!   And a fellow-creature's life hanging in the balance!"

"He doesn't mean it, mother."

"Ah-h-h! yes he does," averred Don Billy. "You don't know 'Nastasie."

Anastasio was running his finger along the

edge of his blade.   First one machete and then
the other was tested in this way; then with a
" Your pardon, Señor," he pulled a coarse hair
from the tail of Don Billy's roan.   This started
the animal kicking; such kicking and plunging
as would have unseated a less experienced rider.

"Y-y-you black rascal!" Don Billy trembled
with rage.   He raised his whip in air.   Anastasio
backed off; showing his teeth he bowed to the
ground.

"I ask ten thousand pardons, Señor."   He
tightened his belt, doffed his hat to the company, and with a machete in each hand, his
powerful arms swinging as he walked, he
started down the path between the rows of
banana trees.

"Where you going, you devil?"

"To kill San José, Señor," smiled Anastasio
back at Don Billy.

"I hope 'Nastasie 'll kill him," said Don Billy,
dismounting.   "He's a sickly little devil.
'Nastasie don't need no machett.   I believe his
lungs is weak.   Hope he'll kill him, anyway!"

"Oh! Mr. Blake, don't say that."

"I'm afraid there's no danger, madam."   Don
Billy mounted the steps on his short, bow legs
and climbed up into the gibbet.   "The fellow's
too far ahead, an' as for me, I ain't in no condition to help chase the darn' Briton.   My head's

dizzy, an' my liver's out of order. My lame leg's a makin' itself heard again, an' my stomach's no good at all; can't even drink a glass of Padre Martinez's pink rum without feelin' it. My lungs are almost utterly useless, an' my heart beats — "

"So does mine, Don Billy. Spare us your organ recital, I beg of you. I thought that I had left those behind in that centre of music from which I hail."

Winton mounted the vacant gibbet, and screwing his eyes into slits, he watched Anastasio's giant form until it was lost among the palms that fringed the plantation.

Anastasio hastened with long strides down the hill. He walked until he came to the bodega. There he stopped and went in. He asked the padre for some bread and a flask of rum. Anastasio had no money, but he told Padre Martinez that he would work out the value of the food when he returned from his man hunt. The Padre Martinez, knowing Anastasio as a man of his word, gave him what he asked for.

"I should hesitate to kill a man, were he black or white," said the padre. "I have but lately had an experience. Oh! but an experience! I know what it is to be killed. I beg of you do not kill him."

"I think that I shall kill him," said Anastasio,

smiling placidly. "The earth has no need of such as he."

"Nevertheless, do not kill him. Turn out his pockets if you will, but do not take a man's life."

Anastasio smiled a pleasant " buen' dia'," and strode away. He leaped across the little stream that flowed near the bodega, and struck into the path that led to the vega. The night grew dark, there was no moon, and after wandering blindly along the rough way he lay down to sleep. The day was yet young when he arose. San José was then more than forty-eight hours ahead of him ; should he catch him ? that was the question in Anastasio's mind. The morning dew stood on the banana leaves in great globules, and rolled like a bit of quicksilver if Anastasio but touched a leaf in passing. The carpenter birds thrust out their heads from holes in the dead palm tree. Anastasio struck the tree several resounding blows as he passed by. The parrots screamed as they flew down toward the delta, a variegated flock of color.

It was not long before Anastasio was well up into the hills. He left the cattle farm upon his left, and now there was nothing ahead for miles but an unbroken grassy plain, the vega of which fearsome tales were told ; the vega crossed and recrossed by paths so many and so winding that

a man must know it well to find his way, the tall
grass hiding from sight all paths but the one
the traveller was himself pursuing. Anastasio
walked with great strides. With a machete in
either hand he swished and cut off the heads of
grass and tall weeds, imagining them always the
head of San José. He met many cattle roaming
wild. Don Felipe counted his cattle by the
thousands; people said that he did not know
how many he owned.

Anastasio knew the vega fairly well, and when
the sun was high he sat himself down by a little
spring of which he knew, and ate some of the
coarse food that he had bought at the bodega.
He had no cup, but he lay down and drank from
the spring, and then he drank a little rum from
his bottle, took another drink of water, and
was off again. That night Anastasio reached a
small belt of woodland, and lying down he slept
until the early mocking-bird awakened him. A
modest bit of food sufficed, and again he started
on.

When Anastasio had been walking about an
hour, over the tops of the tall grass he saw a
horseman coming toward him. As the rider
drew near, Anastasio saw that it was Don Hilario. He was probably coming overland from
"The City" to visit Don Felipe at the cattle
farm. Some persons said that he was to marry

the Señorita Carlota. Don Hilario was close upon Anastasio before he perceived him.

"Oh, is that you, 'Nastasie?" exclaimed Don Hilario, in his perfect Spanish.

"It is I, Señor," replied Anastasio, in his mongrel tongue. "Has the Señor met any one?"

"No one," said Don Hilario. "Or stay, I did meet a man last evening on the other side of the trocha, beyond the hut of Blanco, the Mexican."

"Did you know him, Señor?"

"Yes; I think that he is the Englishman who built the road at the Brandon colonia."

"Ah!" laughed Anastasio, "I am on the right path, then."

"What do you want with him, 'Nastasie?"

"Me?" Anastasio looked up and showed his splendid teeth. "I want to kill him, Señor."

"What has he done to you, 'Nastasie?"

"He has gone off with my money, Señor; thirteen good Mexican dollars, for which I worked these many days."

"I wouldn't kill him, 'Nastasie, for thirteen dollars."

Anastasio was lost in admiration of Don Hilario's fine riding-boots and the long spur on his right heel. He also examined critically the fine leathern belt which Don Hilario wore, the pistols that he carried, and the handsome fowling-piece that was slung over his shoulder. As they stood talking, a large coco flew overhead.

" How far away is he, 'Nastasie?"

Anastasio measured the distance carefully with his eye.

" About fifty yards, Señor."

Don Hilario brought his fowling-piece quickly to his shoulder, and, turning as the bird turned, he suddenly fired. The bird fell a few rods away. Anastasio plunged into the tall grass like a giant retriever, and brought the coco to Don Hilario, who smiled and said : —

" A trophy for Don Felipe."

Anastasio smiled too. He knew very well who would receive that trophy.

" How were they all at the cattle farm as you passed by, 'Nastasie?"

" I did not stop; it was early; but they are well, or I should have heard. Buen' dia', Señor. I should not have stayed so long."

Don Hilario smiled. A sudden conviction came into the mind of Anastasio that he had been purposely delayed.

" Buenos dias, 'Nastasie." They parted, — Anastasio on his quest of murder, Don Hilario on his quest of love.

When Anastasio had proceeded about a hundred yards, he heard a shout. He turned. Don

Hilario had wheeled his horse half-way round, and was sitting sidewise across the path, and looking his way.

"I wouldn't kill him if I were you, 'Nastasie," he shouted.

Anastasio smiled sweetly back at him.

"I must, Señor," he answered; "it is my errand," and went on.

Anastasio turned several times to look at Don Hilario; for the feeling of having a human being near is pleasant upon the vega. There it is as lonely as the Great Desert, and one loses one's way quite as easily; for the grass is tall, the cattle-paths cross and recross each other in a hundred directions, and, while the traveller is following one, another is seldom seen. Even Anastasio, who had been a cattle-tender for Don Felipe, was puzzled at times; and, at the end of the second day, he became anxious. He could not find the spring which he expected to find, and the water in his bottle was gone. Anastasio was a fast walker; he had come a great distance, and yet he had not lost sight of a mountain peak which should have sunk from his view if he was as far on his way as the distance travelled should have taken him. He was overcome with the most burning thirst. He wandered this way and that; he ran at times, and then fell, exhausted, suffering more deeply than before.

Suddenly his strength gave out. It would be prudent to rest awhile, he thought; the sun was fiercely hot; perhaps when it grew cooler he could remember better where to go to find the spring. He stooped down in the path, made a hole in among the tall growth, and crawled into it, pulling the grass over his body, thus sheltering himself from the heat; and then he slept. Anastasio was awakened by a sound near. He sat up, and looked about him. There was nothing to be seen. He stood up and turned his head this way and that. The sound was repeated. It seemed like a human voice not far away. And then, upon his right, but a few paces distant, he saw the grass in motion. He walked toward the spot.

"Water!" he heard; "water!"

He drew near and knelt down; and, in a shelter much like the one that he had made for himself, he saw a man lying on the ground. He opened his eyes, and looked at Anastasio. The man was San José. When he saw Anastasio, San José said: —

"You, 'Nastasie! Why are you here?"

"I have come to kill you," said Anastasio.

"Thank you," answered San José. He spoke with difficulty, and ended with some rambling words.

Anastasio removed his machete from his belt.

o

He ran his finger along the edge of the blade. The steel flashed in the white rays of the sun, and across the eyes of San José. Anastasio saw that the man's swollen lips moved.

" What is that you say ? "

" Be quick ! "

"When he is dead, I will turn out his pockets," thought Anastasio.

What ! rifle the body of the dead ? A slight shudder shook the giant frame of the man.

" Turn out your pockets," said he.

San José looked up inquiringly, and, at a repetition of the order, made a slight gesture indicative of his inability to comply with it.

" Water first. A little water before you kill me," he whispered.

And then memory came to soften Anastasio's heart. He remembered a day last autumn when he had walked many a weary mile, and, coming to Brandon's colonia, he had found a fire, and supper cooking at the rancho. San José was there, and Anastasio was as welcome as any longed-for guest. He remembered the stew, and the crackers, and the hot tea which the Englishman shared with him. Oh, for a sip of that tea now !

" Take all ! only water, for the love of God ! Water, 'Nastasie ! "

Somehow the diminutive of his name, pro-

nounced by this helpless creature, the memory
of the scene at Brandon's colonia, and, above
all, the appeal for water before he should kill
his victim, reached a tender spot somewhere in
the heart of Anastasio. This man was dying
for want of water, and he, Anastasio, talked of
money. He choked; he tried to moisten his
parched lips; his eyes were wet.

"You shall have water if I die to get it," he
said. He ran out into the path, cutting and
slashing at the grass as he went, that he might
find his way back to the spot. He ran hither
and thither, searching in all directions; his
own thirst was beginning to tell terribly upon
him. No water! No water! An hour was
spent in this vain search. He must return,
else San José would die alone.

When Anastasio returned, the man was delirious. He did not recognize Anastasio. He
talked of Lincolnshire and "the rain, the rain,
the blessed rain." His head was burning; he
muttered thickly, he rolled from side to side;
and as Anastasio watched him he rolled over and
directly into a pool of water near which he had
been lying all the time, — a pool which the thick
stalks of the vega-grass had hidden. There was
little of it, and it was not cool, but he pulled the
weeds away and wallowed in it; laid his head
in it, and drank thirstily of the muddy fluid.

Anastasio lay down beside him, and between them they literally drained the little pool dry. Then Anastasio raised San José upon his shoulders and started on his homeward way. He walked until nightfall, stumbling on through blind paths. That evening he was no nearer a spring, and San José rolled restlessly in waking delirium, and called for water, or talked again of Lincolnshire and the blessed rain. When morning broke, Anastasio looked heavenward for the slightest sign of a shower, but the sky was clear and cloudless and the sun arose a ball of fire. Anastasio again raised San José and walked on. His reasoning powers seemed failing; he could not think; he could not recall any guide or landmark by which to remind himself of the way to the spring. As thus he walked the second hour, his mouth dry, parched, San José's delirious murmur in his ear, he heard a sound. A faint " tinkle-tinkle " it was, but it meant life! With renewed energy he stumbled on with his burden toward the place from which the sound arose. The cattle were going to the spring; he had only to follow them.

Don Billy Blake stopped at Don Felipe's cattle farm one early morning.

" Ah, Don Hilario! Is that you? Come from 'The City,' hey? See anything of 'Nastasie as you come along? He's after San José; hope he'll kill the rascal!"

Don Hilario took off his fine Panama and made Don Billy a sweeping and very low bow.

"I gave him opposite advice from the Señor, Don Billyblake, but I doubt if he came up with San José. There are so many paths, and San José was so much in advance. Indeed, I kept 'Nastasie a half hour or more, hoping that he would miss San José. It's an awful thing to kill a man, Don Billyblake."

Don Hilario looked sadly at the colono as he spoke. Rumor had it that he had once killed a man in self-defence out on that very vega. "An awful thing to take a man's life," he repeated.

"Hope he'll kill the dam' rascal all the same! I'm goin' with Don Carlos to look for my brindle' bull. If 'Nastasie has give' up the chase, he may help us find him."

Winton rode his big black horse, Don Billy rode his little roan. At the end of the second day, after a wandering search for the missing bull, Winton and Don Billy turned a corner and suddenly came upon two men. They were sitting in the road, or rather Anastasio was sitting in the road leaning against a tree, and lying beside him, with his head on Anastasio's knee, was San José. Anastasio was gaunt and lean; his food had been gone for several days. San

José was emaciated almost beyond recognition. He talked ever in a thick whisper of Lincolnshire and the rain. Winton saw at a glance the condition of the men.

"Quick, man, your brandy-flask! No! no food; the brandy."

Winton knelt down by the Englishman, hurriedly removing the stopper from Don Billy's flask as he did so. He tried to let a little of the brandy trickle down San José's throat.

"Poor little devil! I told you he hadn't got any staminy," sniffed Don Billy. "Here's food, 'Nastasie."

Anastasio turned away his head. The thought of food made him sick.

"The spring is only a half mile back of us. We must get him there at once," said Winton.

Anastasio, with cracked and parched lips, whispered : —

"Try to live, San José. See! here is food and drink. Water is near, San José; everything!"

San José gave a wild laugh.

"'Nastasie is going to kill me," he said, "for money, for money! Oh, God! Water, water! Give 'Nastasie all the money. Just a little water, a little water, for the love of God! Why, it's Lincolnshire! I — hear it rain! The — rain! The — blessed — rain!"

" Try to live, San José ; water is near."

Don Billy blew his nose upon a green and yellow handkerchief. Then he and Winton stooped and put their arms under San José. They tried to seat him upon the horse, but he fell back into Anastasio's arms.

" Oh ! to — be — home — in — Lin — coln — shire —"

It was like a clock running down. Winton turned away his head.

"In — Lin — coln — shire —— in —— Lin —— coln —— "

The clock had run down.

Anastasio laid his head down on San José's face, and sobbed like a child.

CORNDEAU

CORNDEAU

CORNDEAU was walking along the railway
track, lifting high his black toes to avoid the
thistles which grew between the ties. Corndeau
wore a belt of black with yellow squares which
he had bought at Padre Martinez's bodega. In
this belt he had thrust boastfully two machetes
and a pistol, which he had bought of the captain
of the fruit steamer.

The pistol had cost four dollars, Mexican;
one of its faults was that when the chambers
revolved they did not rest opposite the barrel.
This fact might have caused Corndeau some
inconvenience had he attempted to fire the pistol; as yet he had had no cause to do so.

Over Corndeau's shoulder was slung a gun
with the barrel somewhat bent. His machetes
had just been sharpened on the Señor Don
Billy's grindstone. Corndeau carried a game-
cock under his arm. The cock was a fine one.
It had won seven battles running. Among
them, one from the Alcalde's big red cock, one
from Juan Medina's black cock at Haldez, and

the last one from the pure white cock of the priest at Puerto la Mar. The priest's white cock had been called, regardless of sex, Maria Maddalena, but Maria Maddalena had been a pure white corpse since Sunday, and Corndeau was seeking new fields to conquer.

Coming toward him Corndeau saw a boy. The boy was Franci. Franci also lifted high his yellow toes to avoid the thistles. Franci also had a game-cock under his arm. Franci's game-cock was yellow, and his tail was variegated. He had lost one eye in a fight, but the one remaining was as good as two pair. Franci also had a belt. His belt was white with blue stripes, but, unlike Corndeau, he had no pistol, no machete, and no gun. As the man and the boy were going in opposite directions, naturally in the course of time they met each other.

" Buen' dia'," said Corndeau.

" Buen' dia'," returned Franci.

The cocks exchanged greetings by striking out, each with a spur, and lowering angry heads.

" You laike faight youah cock ? " asked Corndeau, who spoke English imperfectly, and no other language either perfectly or imperfectly.

" Yaas, A' laike," answered Franci.

A man overhead, who had been sawing from a tree a limb which cast too much shade upon the banana patch at the side of the track, was

resting up there in the shady crotch, quietly
eating his breakfast. He dipped his hand into
a pail which hung from a near-by limb. He
filled his mouth with beans and rice; rice that
one sees the world over, beans, the common red
beans of the country. His arm was lame from
sawing through the limbs of the rompe hache.[1]

The previous week Pedro Bolero's gambling
house down at the coast had been closed by
order of the Alcalde, because like his prototype,
Ananias of old, he had kept back part of the
price, and to carry out the likeness to that rec-
reant dealer in real estate he had lied about it.
Pedro Bolero had reported to the Alcalde only
half the gains, and the keen-eyed Alcalde, having discovered a shortage in some other usually
fruitful revenues, had decided that a mild lesson
might have a salutary effect. Hence the erst-
while gambler was at the moment employed in
cutting and lowering branches for the "Big
Company," at the sum of one dollar and thirty-
five cents per day, Mexican. Pedro Bolero
reasoned thus with himself: —

"What was one dollar thirty-five cents
— Mexican — compared with fifty dollars a
day — gold? But what would you have?
The Alcalde had 'recommended' him. There
was no more to be said. He would take good

---

[1] Literally, hatchet-breaker.

care that the Alcalde received a good half, if
ever he got back to Caño Sandros. Oh, yes,
a good half; for even a small half is better than
no bread. Beans and rice!" The hand of
Pedro Bolero made another dip and filled his
mouth. "Paugh! they were not bread. Yes,
decidedly a good half must the Alcalde have."
Pedro Bolero cast his eyes downward to the
shady spot beneath him. A man and a boy
were standing there.

"Youah t'ink you laike faight?" asked the
man.

"Ah t'ink," responded the boy.

"Ma cock kill youah hen."

Franci's soft eyes flashed fire at this speech
of Corndeau's. Dire insult to be wiped out
only by the vanquishment and sudden death
of that brown cock of Corndeau's.

"Youah bate?" inquired Franci.

Corndeau nodded.

"Yaas, Ah bate."

"Bate much?"

"Bate dolla' sev'ty-fy."

"Ho!" Franci's tone rang replete with scorn.
"*Ah* bate ten dolla'."

"Put heem up."

Franci deliberately drew from inside his worn
blue cotton shirt a small red bag in which rattled
ten Mexican dollars. Corndeau's eyes glittered.

"All ri'; let um go."

But Franci held his game-cock firmly in hand.

"Youah money!"

Corndeau raised his sparse eyebrows.

"Ah don' mus' put up. Ah haf ze dolla's, youah haf ze dolla's; let um go!"

But Franci stood stolid.

"*Youah put up!*"

Corndeau laid his hand threateningly upon his machete.

"*Youah put up!*" reiterated Franci, firmly, not even winking.

There was a rustling in the branches overhead.

"Waal! Ah put up — no need. Ma cock kill youah hen, but Ah put up." Out from Corndeau's machete sheath came five greasy United States greenbacks. Franci turned away and started down the track with his cock under his arm.

"Ah luk fo' money."

"Ain' it money what Ah show?"

"Ah not pick dose up 'long a de road! Ah depart."

"Youah return! Ah show de dolla's."

Franci hesitated. The chink of silver persuaded the ear, though the eye could prove nothing as yet. Then out they came: ten shining silver dollars fresh from the bank at Puerto la Mar — dollars which César Palandro had lost his life over the last Saturday night. Franci came back and faced Corndeau.

"Let youah cock go; youah see how quick he dade."

"Won'd battles?" asked Corndeau. He held firmly on to his own brown cock.

"Won'd seven; dis one be eight."

"Nevah won'd no mo'," said Corndeau, solemnly.

"Youah put dere on cleared ground," said Franci. "Ah gif de word."

"No, Ah gif de word."

"No, Ah gif de word."

"No, Ah —"

Suddenly a mocking-bird's whistle was heard; it sounded overhead. Franci looked upward. The boy fancied that he saw a rustling among the branches of the gri-gri tree. Could there be ghosts in the daytime then?

"When mock-bird sing again, we set down."

A nod of acquiescence from Corndeau. They moved about, facing each other, waiting for the whistle. Man and boy grasped, each one, his cock firmly, ready to release it at the chosen signal. It was difficult for Pedro Bolero to whistle with his mouth full of beans and rice. He waited until he saw that Franci had the advantage of sun and position; then his mocking-bird's note trilled sweetly out.

"Put down!" shouted Franci. "Let um go it, Gallagher!"

To what far-away shores will drift some bursts of useful eloquence! Down went the birds, and down went the bird. One blow from the sharp steel on the leg of Franci's cock, and Corndeau's pride lay prone.

"My hen pritty good hen," grinned Franci. "Youah gif my dolla's!"

"No, it was cheat!" screamed Corndeau. "Youah gif my dolla's!"

"Ah gif youah dolla's? No! Ah gif youah good swiff kick ——!"

Corndeau's hand was laid upon his machete; Franci sprang aside. There was a rustling in the branches overhead among the gri-gri leaves, and a sudden trembling below in a young terror-stricken heart. There were day ghosts, then, as well as night ghosts.

"Tu-la-lou, tu-la-lae," sang Franci, in a sort of religious incantatory chant, his nervous young voice sounding clear and high.

But no ghost peered down at him; only his guardian's angry face thrust itself out from between the leaves, and then, as Corndeau came rushing at the boy again, a great branch which hung by a thread of bark was severed and dropped. It crashed to the ground, and pinioned the man to the earth.

P

"Youah pay fo' threaten ma waad," said
Pedro Bolero, as he gazed downward at his prostrate foe.   He spoke slowly.

"Youah remain in hospital laikely about
fouah week wid dat laig." He had descended
the giant trunk, and stood showing his teeth
at Corndeau.   "Youah remain in cep' nodder
mont', laikely, an' den mos' laikely w'en Ah
relate to de Alcalde aall youah nuisances, an'
gif heem of my good pink rum f'om de vega,
youah *git!*"

Franci's game-cock jumped up in the branches
over Corndeau's head and crowed.

WHICH OF THREE?

WHICH OF THREE?

HE was in love with himself, and he had no rivals. He walked down the slopes of La Esperanza, between the rows of banana mats, avoiding carefully the young cacao plants, carrying his heavy body with step as light as if he possessed a good conscience. In the statement that in affection for himself he had no rivals, Beau must be excepted. Beau loved Lottimer almost as well as he loved himself. Beau wagged his tail at the familiar swish of the forest-cut cane, recognizing the possibility of a long ramble. He jumped with great leaps into the air, falling to the ground, only to leap afresh.

At the bottom of the slope, Lottimer met Puenti. Puenti was a pleasant-looking, woolly-headed man, with an off eye, and a very open smile, which showed the gold in his brown teeth. He wore a faded pink cotton shirt, and a pair of trousers much stained with the juice of the green banana, — it stains a dark red.

"Buen' dia', Señor," nodded Puenti, smiling.

" Buenos dias," returned Lottimer, with the particularity of the new importation.

"It haaf par-*rot*," said Puenti, pointing to a squawking flock of color which flew past overhead. " Dey arrive."

" I see they do," said Lottimer, shortly, as he watched the strident-voiced, blue and yellow mass alight in a closely woven screen of behuccas, which hung trailing from a giant ceiba tree, which stood half-way up the hill.

" Eef ze Señor Don Michael veel pressent to me hees fine gun, I veel eemploy myself to shoot ze par-*rot*, wherewiz to concoct ze sin coche."

" Sin coche be dam' ! " said Lottimer, pushing on.

" But, Señor Don Michael, ze par-*rot* make so good sin coche ! "

" Yes, with my barley, and my hominy, and my nice white beans that I had sent from God's country to this cursed hole ; with my potatoes and my onions, no doubt it does make a good dish to put into your dam' black Spanish hide, but — "

Puenti raised his hand as if to ward off the insults.

" A es-Spanish hide, what you call heem, cover a es-Spanish heart and a es-Spanish politeness. Haf we not offer you everyzing in ze island when you land among us, Señor ? "

"Offer! Oh, yes, and dam' little I got! '*My house is yours, Señor*,'" mimicking the courteous manner of Puenti's nation, "and how much have I accepted of you? Did I ever put my foot inside of one of your tumble-down old ranchos? Anybody can offer, but I fancy that all the benefits have come from my side."

Puenti waited courteously for the end of this coarse speech. When Lottimer had quite finished and was turning away, the Spaniard raised his hand to command attention. He stood stiffly, without his usual smile.

"Before we part, Señor, my honah compel me to es-state zat Tre' Pelo' 'as broke ze cep'; 'e roam! Zey haf not apprehend heem."

Dictionary knowledge had Puenti, if not pronunciation, like most inquiring foreigners. Lottimer shrugged his shoulders.

"The cep' should be stronger. Escape connived at, probably, by some blanked black thief of a half-breed."

Puenti refused to accept this remark as a personal one. He persisted.

"Señor, 'e roam, 'e es-steal, 'e killsss."

The last letter was hissed through the gold and brown barrier behind the lips of this descendant of the Spanish Dons, as if meaning enough could not be given to the sound.

"Been threatening to kill me, I suppose."

Lottimer laughed, a fearless cruel laugh. "Let him roam," he called back; "I've nothing to steal but bananas, and he don't hanker after the cep' a second time, I'm thinking; and as to killing, the sooner the Spanish niggers kill each other off like the Kilkenny cats, the better for civilized people."

Puenti still refused to allow Lottimer to give to this innuendo a meaning that was personal. His next request showed this.

"And I can lend ze gun?"

"Caramba, hombre! Can't you understand the meaning of words? No! no! no! You can't take that gun! Why, that gun cost fifty pounds in London. I can use it for birds or men; it shoots very well with a cartridge. Now don't you go up to Esperanza and tell Juan Plumeau that I said you might take that gun; for you can't have it, do you hear?"

"Yess, I 'ear," hissed Puenti. "All ze same 'e killsss." But Lottimer had turned his back and was swinging down the rough road, swearing with eloquence when he caught his foot in an occasional root, or when he splashed himself with the muddy water of a pool.

Puenti stood looking after the owner of La Esperanza. A heavy shower came down upon him without warning. Puenti broke a large banana leaf from the mat nearest him, and held

it over his head. The drops rattled like a fusil-
lade of musketry against the corded surface, and
glittered to the ground. Then the rain ceased
as quickly as it came. Puenti threw his banana
leaf into the suddenly arisen torrent at the side
of the road; it boiled away to the plain.

"All ze same, 'e killsss," hissed Puenti, nod-
ding his head with an impressive smile, as he
saw Lottimer's broad back vanish among the
mompoias.[1] Then he turned and went up to
the casa.

Lottimer continued upon his way. He crossed
the narrow gauge track whose ties were almost
hidden by the weeds which grew between them.
They had not been mowed of late by their gar-
dener — the engine of the fruit train. The train
appeared at La Esperanza with great regularity
as often as once in every two weeks. It came
for its load of bananas; to-morrow would be the
day. All the fruit that was ready had been cut
and piled by the side of the track. Lottimer
stopped and examined critically the great green
mass. There were seven, eight, nine, ten, eleven
and some twelve hand bunches. Not as many
of the latter as he could have wished. They
were covered with large leaves from their own
plants; leaves were laid carefully between the
layers and upon the ground, under those at the

[1] A coarse species of banana.

bottom. They would be packed with as much care into the box cars that would come for them on the morrow, and again into the fruit steamer in the same way, after the inspector had "passed" those that were satisfactory.

"Mighty few eleven and twelve hand bunches," growled Lottimer.

Reaching the narrow path on the further side of the track he struck deep into the heart of the tropical forest. Corkscrews of wood, which once had been green and tender vines, but now had grown to the size of a man's arm, wound from the ground at the side of the path to the branches fifty feet overhead. Scarlet air plants pushed their blossoms in his very face; the two were rivals in color. A black spider crawled out of his path, a scorpion ran across and hid its green body under a leaf. Beau whirled and careered through the foot-deep leaves, burrowing like a mole; scampering periodically back to his master, who as promptly kicked him into the leaves again, from whence he emitted a patient ki-yi, in the Spanish of the island, and returned for another chastisement. The parrots swung and chattered among the swaying screens of vine and flower; the birds sang overhead.

Lottimer pounded along at a furious pace, plunging sometimes into the muddy footprints that a bull had made, splashing his old cotton trousers to the knee. After passing through a mile of forest, he came out upon a small clearing. Here stood a house built of palm boards, and thatched with yagua. The uprights stood upon the ground, the uneven earth making the floor. Lottimer walked along the muddy path to the rough, sunken rock placed there for an entrance step. He kicked away two fowls which were tearing a centipede apart by head and tail, pushed aside the stiff bull's hide curtain, which hung before the entrance of the hut, and entered. At his entrance a dark, Spanish-looking woman arose from her sitting posture before the fire, where an iron kettle was steaming. She faced Lottimer, standing in front of the kettle, as if to screen it from his gaze. Her back was to the fire; the glare shone through her one thin garment.

" So you will steal my fruit, will you ? " snarled Lottimer, savagely.

He advanced threateningly, with his hand upraised; the woman did not quail.

" No tengo," said she, sullenly.

" You haven't, eh ? Look at that, and that, and that ! " As he spoke, he kicked aside the skins of green bananas which had fallen to the floor.

" No, no," insisted the woman; " get f'om Señor Don Billy. Señor Don Billy, he gif fi'-han' bunch."

"Billy·Blake isn't giving away any bananas, that I know of, nowadays, five-hand or any other." Lottimer walked to the further corner of the fireplace. He turned over some leaves with his foot, and brought to light a thick, uneven stalk. "Five-hand bunch, be dam'!" he said; "do you call that a five-hand bunch?"

He raised the crooked stalk and twirled it in front of the woman's eyes, counting aloud, as he pointed to the alternate sides.

"One, two, three, four, five, six, seven, eight, nine, ten. You were not smart, my dear; you should have cut the stalk in two and blackened the cut; then you might have talked of five-hands. Even then, I think I should have caught you. No one ever gets ahead of Michael Lottimer. No, no! Into the cep' you go." He whirled quickly round, his great weight making a heel-mark in the earthen floor.

"Who've you got in there?" He pointed toward the inner room. The woman stretched out her hands, as if to warn him off.

"Nada!" she said in native Spanish. "Nada, nada!"

He started toward the bull's hide which hung in front of the second entrance. With a lithe movement she planted herself before it.

"No entre," she said fiercely. She glared defiance at Lottimer. For answer, he laughed

contemptuously, tore the skin from its fastening.
It fell to the floor.   Upon a bed of grass, in the
further corner of the room, lay a man, hollow-
eyed and gaunt, shaking with a chill.   His skin
showed a strange pallor which one never sees in
a white victim of the calentura.

"So!   Tre' Pelo', you are again out of cep';
you roam, you steal, you kill, eh?"

"No, no! Señor Don Michael; 'tengo calentura."

"Fever, bosh! who told you that you might
occupy this rancho?   I'd kick you out now, only
when the police come they may as well take
you both."

"Oh! Señor, Señor! Not a de cep', not a de
cep'! Luk, Señor Don Michael."

From under the wilted banana leaf, which was
their only covering, the man thrust forth two
feet which were swollen and black; the ankles
ringed with the marks of the stocks.

"Ha! I like to see that! shows there's some
justice, even in this black hole."   He gave the
prostrate man a kick, made another wheel in
the floor, and went out.   There was emitted
from between Tres Pelos's trembling and nearly
closed eyelids a gleam of hatred, which it would
have been well for Lottimer to see.   Beau the
friendly drew near, and sniffed at Tres Pelos,
but came flying through the doorway after his
master, sending forth a succession of shrill yelps.

When Lottimer turned, Dolores was standing in the doorway, her dark eyes flashing, a machete in her hand, a pistol in her belt. "So that's your game! You see that I am unarmed. Well, my pretty dear, I shall laugh last and longest." And then followed a volley of oaths.

The curtain is perhaps among the most convenient and useful works of man. Where there is no hope of either prevention or cure, the only refuge is secrecy. Let us hasten to draw a sound-proof curtain before the master of La Esperanza, although by so doing we efface much of the local color. When Lottimer had plunged back into the forest, Dolores looked in at Tres Pelos.

"He lif too long already," said she.

The man, aided by a chill, nodded his acquiescence.

The sun was setting as Lottimer returned through the woods. Beau bounded ahead, an ever-palpitating silhouette against the gold. The tropical night had fallen as he entered the mompoia patch at the foot of the hill. Arrived at the house, Juan Plumeau came out to the veranda to meet him.

"Misser Puenti he been here. He red-hot cultivator, Misser Puenti. He want fo' lend Señor Don Michael pick."

"Did you give it to him?"

"Yaas, Señor; gif him pick, an' agopete.[1] Señor Don Michael promise him."

"The devil you did! I told Puenti distinctly that under no circumstances could he take my gun. You black scoundrel, I believe you are all in league! I dare say you'd like to kill me, but I'm not afraid of forty such niggers as you."

Juan Plumeau's three drops of Spanish blood boiled up in wrath, but his inheritance from servile fathers persuaded him to maintain a respectful silence; besides, he wished to ask a favor.

"Is my dinner ready?"

"Si, Don Michael," ultra humility in the tone.

The dinner was served and eaten upon the veranda.

"You are failing in your cooking, Juan Plumeau," remarked Lottimer, as he trickled the black coffee down from his spoon. "That sin coche wasn't half as good as usual."

"Si, Señor. Señor Puenti, he say —"

"Damn Señor Puenti!"

"Si, Señor, damn him!" assented Juan Plumeau, politely. "He say —"

"I don't want to hear anything about what he says. You finish your dishes as soon as you can. I have something for you to do."

[1] Agopeta, or ecopete, a corruption of the Spanish word *escopete*, shot-gun.

"If the Señor allow, I like to go to the gambling at the bodega to-night."

"You can't go. I have other things for you to do." Lottimer caught a cuculla and put the brilliant creature inside a tumbler. He watched it crawl up the glass and fall, after each effort, to the table. The illuminations of head and body made a lamp of the tumbler. "What are you waiting for? I want you to start for Haldez as soon as you have finished your work. Do you hear?"

"Si, Señor." Juan Plumeau's tone contained a hidden joy. "Was not the bodega on the way to Haldez?"

"And you go direct to the Alcalde, Juan Plumeau, and you tell him that you come from me, and that I want two big policemen over here by daybreak."

"Si, Señor."

"I'll have Tre' Pelo' and his woman in the cep' before to-morrow night."

"Si, Señor." Juan Plumeau's tone was not quite so pleasant. Dolores was the sister of Juan Plumeau.

"Oh, you needn't look at me that way! I ain't afraid of a whole regiment of you Spanish niggers."

"The Señor will be alone all of the long night."

"Alone!" Lottimer laughed. "Come, get on with you!"

"Can I accommodate myself upon the little black horse of the Señor Don Michael?"

"You cannot. You can accommodate yourself upon your two black legs. The river is low; you can ford; and mind that you are back by daylight." Lottimer sat and smoked and ruminated. He heard Juan Plumeau rattling his dishes, — slopping the water over the kitchen floor, from whence it poured in a waterfall down over the high steps. "Hurry up, Juan Plumeau! No time for dinner; eat and run!" Could he have seen the savage glare of Juan Plumeau's eye! At last Lottimer heard the sharp slam and the locking of the kitchen door, and the sound of Juan Plumeau's horny feet pattering down the hill. He heard, also, a "Buen' noch', Señor," but he saw neither the tipping of the old Panama hat, — remnant of Spanish veneer, which had become second nature with the serving class, — nor did he catch the glance of hatred which flashed from under the brim. "Don't you stop at Tre' Pelo's!" shouted Lottimer. "Go right along now!" But no answer came back to him. Perhaps Juan Plumeau had gone too fast and too far to hear the command.

Lottimer sat puffing his cigarillo. The trade-wind, softened into a tender breeze by the fall

Q

of night, fanned his coarse red cheek. The banana leaves rustled. A cloud floated across the
moon, which looked through its long fleece-edged
cracks and made their edges bright for the
time. The cucullas flew about the lamp, or
walked by twos and threes up the veranda wall.
The lizards squeaked faintly as they scurried
along the rafters, or peeped down with watchful
eyes, set in pointed green heads, at Señor Don
Michael. The late nightingale tipped a stave,
and the mocking-bird answered from the top of
the dead palm tree. There was a sound as of
a rat moving stealthily underneath the house.
There was room for the rat, for the pilotillos
upheld the flooring at ten feet from the
ground.

Beau barked out into the night. Lottimer
looked out there as if his eyes could penetrate
the darkness. There was nothing to be seen,
only the near great banana fringes waving in
the breeze. The place was a lonely one, — a
plantation quite away from other colonias. Lottimer would have laughed had any one asked
him if he was afraid. He never had felt even
lonely before; but it was a place remote from
human companionship, and suddenly he seemed
to appreciate this fact. Back of the house, up,
up, up the hill, stretched the forest primeval;
below, and far away on each side, stretched the

thousands of waving fruit trees. Beau barked incessantly.

"Stop that!" said Lottimer, fiercely. He kicked the little animal the length of the veranda, where he was stopped by the water cask. His yelp of pain made Lottimer more nervous than before. He seemed to take comfort in talking to the animal. "Come! go into the house; it's my bedtime if it isn't yours. In with you." The cowed creature slunk into the room where his master slept.

Lottimer closed and barred the door and shutter; he did the same in the second room. He looked up at the rafters of this room.

"I wonder where they think I keep the silver," he said, half aloud. "Of course they know I can't go to Puerto la Mar before every pay day." He looked at the sea-chest resting upon the rafters, a chest painted lead color, with beckets for handles.

Beau was barking violently in the sleeping-room. Lottimer went in angrily, and found the dog with his nose to a broad crack in the floor. A kick sent the beast to his corner. Lottimer lifted a demijohn from the table, and pouring a tumbler half full of liquid drank it off. He then diluted it internally from the water-monkey, and undressing threw himself heavily upon his cot. He lay looking at the bright streaks that the moonlight made as it crept through the spaces beneath the rafters, under the eaves.

That rat again!

Beau still growled and sniffed at the crack in the floor.

"Go to sleep, you brute!" growled Lottimer.

The wind arose. It sighed and moaned. The tall banana tree at the corner of the veranda tap-tapped upon the roof as if in warning. The dog crawled out from his corner and crouched along to the side of the bed, not quite sure of his welcome, yet recognizing something kinder in his master's tone. He licked the hanging hand inquiringly, and then scrambled unforbidden upon the bed. He lay there starting and whimpering, and at intervals sniffing the air. Sometimes he jumped to the floor, put his nose to the crack and barked, unheeded by his now unconscious master.

The banana leaf tap-tapped upon the corner of the roof.

At about three o'clock two shots rang out in quick succession, but Juan Plumeau, if he were returning from Haldez, could not have heard them, for he must have been at least three miles away. The colonias all about were wrapped in slumber.

At daybreak a crowd of curious men stood upon the veranda and filled the casa at La Esperanza. Some one had broken down the door of what had been Lottimer's room. The bullets had bored two holes in the thin flooring before puncturing the canvas of the cot. The lead-colored chest was upon the floor of the second room, open and empty. Lottimer's gun was upon the floor, also empty. A silver dollar had rolled into a corner, sticking fast in a crack. This was claimed by the Alcalde as his perquisite. The only regret at La Esperanza was shown by a little dog. He sat whining upon the floor, and licked the lifeless hand which hung down over the edge of the cot.

"His agopete; zat killsss," hissed Puenti, as he kicked the empty gun out of the way.

PLUMERO THE GOOD

PLUMERO THE GOOD

The Padre Martinez had lost all the honest earnings which had come to him from the last cockfight—for even the winnings at a cockfight may be honest ones. Added to this, the good padre had nearly lost his life; hundreds of dollars — Mexican — had been staked and lost.

The cockfight at Padre Martinez's bodega had rivalled a gala night at the far-famed gambling establishment of Pedro Bolero at Caño Sandros. As much money changed hands at one as at the other. When Pedro Bolero opened the doors of his Casa de Juego, one always knew who would be the winner at the end of the evening; but with regard to the cockfight, one could not predict so surely. All cocks might enter the lists, and it was just possible that some feathered thing with sharp spurs and a wary eye could be found to beat the cock of the Padre Martinez; but no one was ever known to come off victorious where Pedro Bolero was concerned; therefore cockfighting, because it possessed an element of doubt, was made doubly exciting.

All the hundreds of dollars which had been lost, had first been won by a cock with as many colors as Joseph's coat, and with names to match. The first of these names the historian has forgotten; the list ended, regardless of gender, with a melange which began with Juan Maria and ended with Isabella Fernando Cristoforo Colon Martinez. This bird of multiple colors and cognomens had won his last fight. But first he had sent the cock of the Spanish doctor to hell where he belonged; so said Plumero, surnamed The Good. The Spanish doctor took another view of the matter; he averred that his black cock had taken flight for a better land, where all good cocks go. Machetes were drawn and flourished, but the gentle Padre Martinez used the pacific influence of the rum from the vega so liberally that soon Alicante (Plumero the Good) and the little black Spanish doctor were kissing each other through penitent tears.

Then Juan Maria Isabella Fernando Cristoforo Colon Martinez, with one nail torn off and one eye sightless, jumped lamely to the Padre Martinez's shoulder and gave a triumphant, though exhausted, crow; after which he settled down to a well-earned rest in the padre's grateful arms.

"Ah! thou blessed one!" whispered the Padre Martinez to the maker of his fortunes. " Henceforth shalt thou eat of the boiled corn, the ripe banana; and thy drink shall be of the water from my own blue-striped perron. Thou shalt not henceforth consort with the common fowls. Thy names shall be graven upon the door of thy house; they should be inlaid in letters of silver, were it not that such rascals as Carlos Plumero the Bad, and Pedro Garcia still walk the good God's beautiful earth, and they would pick out the letters on the first dark night. See! my Rose from the gardens of Granada, I place thy dollars in the drawer, thy many hundred Mexican dollars. Ah! these winnings are heavy; they take their own time to be secreted. Then I lock the drawer thus, turning the key twice; I then place the key in my pocket. Who is that? thou, Alicante? I am telling Cristoforo Colon that to-morrow I saddle the old Perigo and ride quickly to the bank at Haldez, and there deposit his earnings until such time as we can depart for the land of sunny Spain."

The Padre Martinez kissed the cock's battered head and sat himself down to his simple supper of beans and rice, prepared for him by the hands of Plumero the Good. This native dish was supplemented with a plate of fried bananas, and

helped on its way by a tall glass of rum from
the vega, weakened with pure cold water from
the blue-striped perron; the perron which the
padre had carried overland from "The City" a
hundred miles away.

No one knew how or when it happened.
Early the next morning some peons came to
the bodega with vales from their colonias to
exchange for food. Their ready money had all
been wagered on the black cock. They found
the shutter pried off its hinges and the good
old padre lying stiff upon the floor, bathed in
his own blood. His fingers were clenched, and
from them stood up straight and accusing some
strands of dark bronze-colored hair. Upon the
floor lay an ornament which had dropped or
been broken from a machete handle. It was
plain that there had been a struggle; it was
plain that the thieves had thought themselves
murderers as well, for they had vanished in haste.

The padre was not dead. He could not tell
the story of the attack. He only rolled his eyes
wildly toward the shutter and weakly cried: —

"All, all, gone! My hundreds of dollars!
Robbers! thieves! Silver dollars! Mexican dollars! all, all, gone!"

The many-colored cock had come in for his
share of ill-treatment, and lay weak and helpless in the corner of the bodega. Evidently the

robbers had thought that the hasty twist they gave his neck had ended his life.

Why the word gratitude was invented it is vain to surmise. Why should we retain in our vocabularies a part of speech that has not, that never had, that never will have upon earth, its equivalent in an attribute which can give it reason for existing? The cock had won the fortune, the thieves had profited by his prowess, and, presto! they had wrung his neck, or so they thought. A cock of experience could have expected nothing less.

When the gaping peons had raised the good padre and laid him upon his cot in the inner room, they searched the compact little store, but there was no more evidence to be found, the few reddish hairs and the machete ornament being the silent witnesses of what might have been a tragedy. There was nothing left in the drawer, not even a centavo.

And now Alicante Plumero came hurrying up; Plumero the Good, who lived at the bodega, and attended to the customers when the padre was away. Carlos Plumero, the brother of Alicante, had faithfully earned the sobriquet of " The Bad," and the peons said that Alicante shone by contrast. They declared that the worst criminal in the cep' over at Saltona would shine by comparison with Carlos Plumero, and appear as an archangel beside him. So those colonos who had suffered from Carlos in various ways also believed, but the padre said that they were jealous of his good Alicante, whom he had never found out in a wrong deed.

"Plumero the Good hasn't never broke the eleventh commandment," said Don Billy Blake one day, after a long space of thought, and the saying immortalized him.

Plumero the Good wept with rage when he discovered his old master lying there, almost unconscious.

"The good God strike them dead!" he cried, as he raised his hands to heaven. "The good God hang and drown them. Let one drown and the other hang! So say I."

Don Billy Blake was returning home from a late carouse. He stopped at the bodega for a revivifier, in the shape of a glass of the padre's fine pink rum from the vega. He listened to Plumero the Good, with his head on one side like an old bird. Don Billy did not think very quickly, but his thoughts came along in spots, and were usually to the point when they appeared.

There was a general chorus of "Oh, yes, they must be killed! both must be killed." Don Billy blinked his little eyes.

"How do you know there were two, hombre?"

"I know not if there were one, two, or many,

Señor; but whoever and wherever they are, the good God punish them as they deserve. Hang them! drown them! Anything is much too good. Oh, my poor, poor padre! my poor old master!"

Alicante wept, and beat his head. He tried to lift the padre from the ground where he lay.

"No! no! No one shall touch him but me," he said, as the others offered their help. But the padre's weight was too much for Plumero the Good. And, as the simple peons raised the prostrate man, Don Billy walked close alongside, and thought again. Though Don Billy's eyes were small, they were keen. He bent over the old man, and scrutinized his hands.

"Ah!" exclaimed Don Billy.

"And what is that which the Señor discovers?" questioned Plumero the Good.

"Hairs," replied Don Billy; "three hairs."

"Ah, yes! And is it that I do not know the accusation that you would make, Señor? It is that the hairs match with those of my brother, whom you are pleased to call Carlos the Bad."

Don Billy thought quickly, for him.

"Have you looked at 'em, Alicante?"

"Cannot every one who is present see them in the hand of the good old padre? And if they are of a dark red color, is that any reason to suspect my poor brother?"

"I don't think your brother's been mentioned except by you, Alicante."

"Ah, yes! but I know well what the Señor is thinking."

By this time they had laid the padre upon the bed, and the women who had run in from the nearest colonia were examining his wounds.

"Run for the doctor — the little Spanish doctor."

"Alas! he returned to Puerto la Mar last evening, after the cockfight," said Plumero. And then, turning again to the Señor Don Billy Blake, he said fiercely, "As well accuse me of murdering my beloved master, as to accuse my brother. See! the hairs match also with mine own. Is that any reason that I, who loved him so dearly, should be accused of this awful crime? I would kill any one who hinted at such a thing."

Don Billy's revolver was drawn from his belt. Plumero clapped his hand to his side.

"My machete! Ah, yes! lost this morning, cutting the green bananas for the stew."

One of the peons opened his hand.

"By some chance, was this the ornament of thy machete?"

Plumero the Good looked darkly at the man.

"It is the ornament from the machete of my brother; but what of that? The colinos are many of them alike, or the thief may have stolen his to throw the blame upon him."

Don Billy opened his slits of eyes. Thought had surprised him again.

" If we was in the States where all thieves and robbers get justice, and if I was your lawyer, Plumero the more than Good, I should advise you not to talk."

" And not to talk! I! What have I to be afraid of? But my poor brother! There is an old Spanish saying, 'Give a dog a bad name, and hang him.'"

" I told you not to talk," said Don Billy.

" And not to talk! And not to talk! And are the dark red hairs so rare that the vile robber must be my poor brother?"

Don Billy seemed to have struck a train of persistent thought.

" No one ain't a talkin' about your brother but yourself," he said.

" A hen he will take on occasion; that I do not deny." The peons grinned; they had seen Carlos in the cep' only the past week on the charge of chicken-stealing. " He will not even hesitate at a six-hand bunch, if hungry; but raise his hand against the good old padre, never! Look you, Señor Don Billyblake. Who else has the hairs of the dark red color, who but the Scotch shop-keeper Dugaldo? You

R

smile, you are incredulous! But he also attended the fight of the cocks. His hair is a
match for those that you hold in your hand.
Our father was of the Scotch blood, also; but
he had not a Scotch nature, though the good
God ordered that he gave us also the red hairs.
Is it then because my poor brother has done
some bad actions that he is to be accused of all?
No, no! This time it must be the Dugaldo.
He will cheat in the shop; he will give you a
half-pint less of the pink rum to the gallon than
the law demands. Go to his shop! search him!
but let my poor brother alone."

"You *will* talk," said Don Billy.

The women closed the door of the padre's
room, to keep out the sound of Plumero's voice.

"And are my plans nothing? I had just come
in to ask permission of the good padre that I
might absent myself for a few days. I wish to
go up to the cattle ranch of the Don Felipe; I
wish to marry the daughter of the Don Felipe."

"What you want and what you'll get are two
very different things."

Don Billy had had a second glass, which he
poured from the demijohn behind the counter.
His thoughts came at a gallop for him.

"I shall be gone but a few days, three at the
most; and when my festivities are over I shall
not be too proud to return and serve my old

master, to sell the beans and the rice as heretofore."

The peons looked at one another in surprise.
What was this? Alicante marry the beautiful
Carlota, the daughter of the cattle king Señor
Rodriguez? Could it be? The Señorita had
lovers coming as far as from "The City,"
itself.

" As likely to marry my Inez," growled Luis,
from the canucca down by the river.

Don Billy sniffed and went in to examine the
padre.

" Stop your clack, Alicante," he said as he
came out. " If your brother did begin it, you
will finish it with your everlasting gabble. Out
with you!" Don Billy drew his pistol. The
peons scattered. " And remember what I told
you : don't talk."

Alicante vanished in the path leading toward
the river, and the padre was left to the care of
Inez, and Mercedes from the canucca at the river
patch. Little Cristina poked her head cautiously
in the door as the day wore on, but Mercedes
warned her away and told her that probably
Tomacito had devoured in her absence the five-
hand bunch that was ripening for the coming
week. And the padre was left to the quiet
care of Mercedes and Inez, who talked each one
as soon as the other had stopped, and usually

talked several minutes together without discovering it.

The river ran past the great cattle farm of Señor Don Felipe Rodriguez. The Señorita Carlota lived there with her father. The casa was a collection of rambling buildings, built entirely of palm board, and thatched with yagua, with verandas running in all directions; and wherever the sun was not, and the shade was coolest, there one might find the Señorita on any day of the week, unless she had chosen to ride with her father to see the rounding up of the cattle, or to visit some outlying farm.

Little Arnol was Carlota's factotum. He was too young to do any of the heavy work of the house, but he ran on errands, killed parrots and carpenter birds for the sin coche, snared the cooing dove for broiling, or shot the mocking-bird when he could borrow, unknown to the owner, the Señor Don Felipe's fine gun which had been sent over from London. Arnol had to get very deep into the woods to accomplish this, for the Señorita was sure to hear the gun go off, and then she would examine every bird which Arnol brought in. The doves and parrots she thought were proper prey, but a mocking-bird she would not have Arnol kill if she knew it. Arnol usually picked the mocking-birds in the woods and burned their feathers down by the cocoa drying-house, and then swore that a sweet note never came out of their throats.

"Arnol, haste then! We need the red beans and some rice also. We need some lard, and some of the square sugar for my father's coffee. Haste, then, to the bodega. Here are two Mexican dollars, and what the good Padre Martinez forgives thee of the money, thou canst keep." Arnol's pretty face lighted up like the sun. "But much there will not be." Arnol's face looked like a cloud of darkest hue. "If thou seest some fine fig bananas, thou canst buy them, and a juicy pine and some mangos, for is not Don Hilario coming over from 'The City' to-day or to-morrow, and must we not be ready for so grand a guest?"

Arnol's thick lip stood out beyond his nose. He saw his commission rapidly diminishing.

"If the Señorita allow, I should like a belt for my machete and my pistol. So expensive a pistol needs a strong belt. The Señorita knows that I bought it from the American captain for three dollars and thirty-five cents, Mexican. It is true that he forgot to give me the cartridges, but those he will bring at the next coming of the fruit steamer."

"Very well, then, Arnol. Here, take the book, and what the belt costs must be entered in the account, and shall be deducted from thy next month's wages."

The Señorita smiled, and Arnol knew that not a centavo of his money would ever go towards paying for the pistol belt. He intended to get a red one with squares of yellow, and leathern straps, like the one that Misser Williams wore when he brought the Señora over from Las Lilas. Arnol was all smiles.

" I can take the red pony ? "

" It has gone with Gomez to the clearing."

" I may lend the great gray horse ? "

" Why trouble me with silly questions ? Thou knowest well that he has, in his turn, taken my father, Don Felipe, across to the colonia of the Señor Brandon."

" The Señorita allows that I ride the white bull ? "

" His back is still sore from the aparejo, which that wretched Plumero — "

" Alicante the Good ? — "

" God forbid ! Alicante the Bad. He rode the pretty white bull too hard when he borrowed him one day last week, and my father turned him off the plantation. Besides which, he looked at me as one in his station should not look. I have given Leon the oil and the carbolic, and he washes the place and applies the carbolic with a feather. No aparejo until the bull is better."

"The Señorita will not refuse me the brown bull?"

"He is too vicious for thee, child; besides, he is carrying suckers to the newly avita[1]-ed field; so with the spotted bull and the great black one. But use thy eyes, and ask not foolish questions. Run along! Some one will be coming this way and bring the purchases home. Say that they are for the Señorita Carlota. That is enough. Any one will carry them."

Carlota smiled consciously. She went to a shady corner of the veranda and stretched herself lazily in a hammock. She adjusted her pillow, and took Calderon's poems from a chair near by.

Arnol stood looking gloomily at the Señorita's slippered foot and the sweep of her filmy gown back and forth upon the veranda floor, as the hammock swung this way and that. His face was full of a sulky displeasure. His lips pouted, and the lines of his face were heavy. Thus he communed with himself: —

"The sun is dam' hot; the woods are damp. It is probable that I shall take the calentura, but what cares she if I die? She, with her lovers and her vanity and her old father's money! The old Señor gives her all that money can buy; and for me? — not even a bull. Thou

1 Avita, to clear a field.

good God! A cattle farm, and not a bull to ride to the bodega! Saints in heaven! A cattle farm, and not a bull to spare!"

It was twelve o'clock; the remains of Don Felipe's second breakfast stood upon the table by the front steps — his French coffee pot, his plate of rolls. The sin coche had been cold for some time past, but Arnol dipped a finger in it when Carlota was not looking; so with the glass dish of guava jelly; and hastily gathering up the sugar that yet remained in the bowl, and putting a roll in his open shirt front, he lagged slowly down the steps.

Marita with a great clatter came to clear away the dishes.

"Thou angel of my soul! When wilt thou have thy chocolate? Wilt thou starve thyself until the Don Felipe returns from the Brandon colonia?" Her tone changed as her eyes fell upon Arnol hanging listlessly on to the pilotillo nearest the front steps. "And art thou still here, in thy blackest of black sulks? Hasten then, the Don Hilario may arrive at any moment, and we may need the rice and the beans this very hour."

Arnol looked at the Señorita. She seemed deeply intent on her poems, but a conscious smile played over her features as Marita mentioned the name of Don Hilario.

"She and her Don Hilario, they may starve for me!"

She did not raise her eyes, and Arnol started slowly down the broad hot walk. He followed the main road as long as he was sure that the keen eyes of Marita could detect his form, but when the branching trees hid him from sight, he struck into the wood and made his way toward the river.

"I shall at least save myself a part of this long hot walk," said Arnol. "There lies the boat of Gomez which he has been hollowing from the trunk of a ceiba tree for weeks past. Gomez is none too considerate of me. Now when he wishes his boat he can go and look for it in the flats of the delta, for I shall ride to the ford that is nearest the bodega, and then it may go where it will."

Arnol had a savage love for bright colors, and delighted in making them subserve his flights of imagination. He pulled great crimson blossoms and gigantic yellow lilies from vines which he passed; he tore the single flower from each air plant, and approached the rough boat, his body almost hidden by the gorgeous mass of blooms. Gomez's work, patiently carried on at such times as he could steal away, was fully appreciated by Arnol. He decked the little craft from stem to stern, and when he had made for himself a

bower of color he stepped lightly into the vessel
and laid himself down.

"And now Don Hilario may wait for his rice
and beans! Thou good God! not even a bull!
That was not the treatment that one would
receive in heaven. The good God would provide bulls for worthy boys." Of that he was
sure. He had cut a stick with which to push
himself from shore when he felt so inclined.
He had also cut the broad spatules from a wild
banana tree, and these he bent over himself in an
arch, making thus a perfect screen. A mysteri-
ous green and yellow light shone through the
corded leaves. Arnol had heard of the green
depths of the sea. He listened when on Sunday the Señorita read to her father, the old
Señor, all that the journals contained. Those
journals that were brought by Vapor Cleede,
or else came down from the far North in the
fruit steamer. It seemed to him that he might
be lying in a cave far down in the great ocean.
The light hurt his eyes, he closed them and then
he slept.

Dissipation, which saps stronger constitutions
than little Arnol's, had begun to take revenge
the moment that her master, Law, was out-
raged. The boy was stealing from the day to
repay what he had given to the night. For
Arnol, too, had been at the cockfight, and had

stealthily returned to the cattle farm at midnight, following Gomez and the others for fear
of meeting with a ghost if he took a more lonely
path. He had crept silently away to his hammock up over the stable, and it seemed but a
moment from the time that he laid himself
down until the shrill-voiced Marita called him
again. When Arnol awoke his boat was in
motion. And what was this? Could it be that
the boat was moving? He tore away the leaves
and flowers above his head. Yes, yes, the boat
was moving! Gomez had wondered if she would
float. Well, Arnol could tell him, that is, if he
chose. It was an exciting moment.

"This is fine," said Arnol. "I have nothing
to do but sit and enjoy. The Don Hilario will
think our Señorita a poor housekeeper. Well,
then, so much the better for all of us." Trees,
rocks, banks were skimmed by, and left behind.
A stop for a moment; the boat had struck a
rock, and when she dislodged herself Arnol was
going backward down the stream. Another
bump, and Arnol's boat was high and dry upon
a small island in mid-stream. "I see how it is,"
thought Arnol, "the river is rising." The boy
heard the sawing of branches at Cuba Libre.
He shouted until he was hoarse, but no one
seemed to hear him on that side. He shouted
again. This time his call was answered. He

turned, and looked toward the left bank.   There
stood Inez.   She had the little Laura by the
hand.   Inez hollowed her palm and put it to
her mouth.

"And is that you, Arnol?   And how did you
get there?   Are you sailing on the branch of a
tree?"

"It is no branch of a tree, this upon which I
sail," said Arnol.   "This is a boat.   I am sailing to the bodega."

"Oh, that bodega!" wailed Inez.   The little
Laura put up her lip and began to cry.   Inez
gave her a gently impatient jerk.   "It is my
opinion that thou wouldst cry if thou wert told
that thou shouldst never eat another thing but
sugar-cane."

The little Laura stretched her mouth until she
lost all resemblance to a human being.   The tears
rolled down her cheeks, and dropped upon her
little shirt, — her only garment.   Inez placed
her hand under the child's shoulders, and swung
her up to her hip where she sat astride, — a leg
in front and a leg behind.

"Come and help me push off my boat," called
Arnol.

"The water is deep.   I cannot leave the little
Laura."

"Oh, thou and thy Laura!   I will give thee
and thy Laura a sail in my fine boat."

Inez raised her one skirt and stepped into the flood. Before she had walked a third of the way toward Arnol's island, the water was above her knees. Laura's mouth threatened to crack at the corners, and her tears helped to swell the flood. She shrieked; she threw herself backward. Inez very nearly lost her hold of the frightened child. She turned, and began to walk toward the shore.

"I dare not try to come further, Arnol. I should be drowned, and the little Laura also. I will go home and send Luis to thee."

"Luis!" Arnol's face was convulsed with rage. "I espit upon thee and thy Luis. Thy Luis is even a greater coward than thyself, or even thy skate-fish child. Luis! Luis! Luis!" Each time that Arnol pronounced the name of Luis, he spat upon the water.

"That boat will carry thee away to the sea, child, and to the sharks. The same sharks which ate a Señor named Jonas,[1] so the padre said. Oh, the poor padre!" And Inez wailed again, and Laura's features were crowded up, down, right, and left.

"Much better to be with the sharks than with thee, and thy coward of a Luis, and thy skate-fish child," and Arnol diligently spat upon the surface of the river. When nature refused fur-

[1] Jonah.

ther drain upon an exhausted supply, Arnol laid down upon the sand, and filled his mouth with the river water. He then arose, and, making a hollow of his cheeks, he sent a long thin stream toward Inez. Laura watched this process delightedly. Her features came round from the sides of her head, and she almost smiled. This angered Arnol until he danced on the little sand island, in a paroxysm of rage. " Much rather would I be with the sea and the sharks ! Much ! Much ! "

Arnol watched Inez's form as it rapidly disappeared along the river bank. He shook his small fist at her until he could see her no more; then he turned, and once again got into his boat.

It grew dark, the sun went down, and there came a chill in the air. Arnol sat within the hollowed trunk, and watched the water. A few faint stars came out; their reflections were sprinkled in long, dancing ribbons of light on the surface of the flood. A slight movement! the water was all round the boat now. Ah! she moved! she was off again! Arnol drifted along. He was helpless. There was nothing to do but to remain where he was, and be carried to the sea. So much the better. He would meet a Vapor Cleede down in the great bay of which the Señorita had told him. The American captain would invite him on board. The captain would

take him up to that wonderful country called
"The es-States," which the Señor Don Billyblake
was always talking of. The Señor Don Billyblake called it God's country. Perhaps it was
heaven. He always talked of it when he and
Don Felipe smoked the cigarillos, and drank the
black coffee.

Arnol knew just what he would do when he
arrived in that grand city called Neuva Yorka,
as near as he could remember. It was a city as
large as Caño Sandros, Saltona, and Haldez, all
in one. Arnol would go and join the junta.
Every one would join the junta who had the
chance. And they would give him shoes, —
Arnol looked at his long, yellow toes, — fine
shoes with very high heels, and very short in
the foot, like Don Andrea's, and which hurt the
feet badly, and made one walk like a Señor.
Those shoes would cost, perhaps, as much as two
dollars — Mexican — a pair. And then they
would give him a silk hat, high and black, like
Don Hilario's, and a white shirt with big, purple
spots, — spots nearly as big as a dollar — Mexican. The shirt would have long cuffs which
would come down to his knuckles. They would
also give him a blue-and-white checked coat like
the one that Don Felipe wore when he went to
meet El Presidente at the city. He would have
white trousers, very tight and short, — no ba-

nana stains on them! — and he would have a
large seal ring on his middle finger; and he
would wear a red necktie like Don Billyblake's
best one; and a collar, — oh, yes, he must not
forget the collar, — a very high collar, that, with
sharp points which would stick into his throat;
and he would carry a little brown cane, which
he would twirl round between his fingers; and
he would have a checked case of cigarillos,
which he would offer to the gentlemen of the
junta. And when the president of the junta
told the members that Señor Don Arnol Des-
sange had come all the way north in Vapor
Cleede to offer his services for "Cuba Libre,"
they would put their hands on their breasts, like
those Dons in the Señorita's picture, and he
would take off his high silk hat, draw his right
toe up to his left instep, cast his eyes down with
great humility, and say, "Señores!" That was
the way the priest did when he came up to the
casa. And then he would buy a much finer belt
than the one which he was going to get to-day
at the bodega, and some new colinos, very
sharp and long, and — A bump! the boat had
grounded.

Arnol waked from his sleepless dream. He
peered out; then he stepped cautiously over the
bow in the darkness, and found that he was on
rising ground. He knelt, and felt of the sur-

face on which he stood. It was gravelly. He heard the water rushing along on each side of him; he had landed upon a second island. The boy stood in the darkness, wondering what he should do. As he stood thus, he heard voices. They came from in front, from down the river. He was about to shout, when he heard the name that he loved best in the world. It was "Carlota." Who could these persons be who spoke so freely of his beloved Señorita?

"When she sees all this money, she will marry me, and no other."

There seemed to be a glow of light somewhere ahead. It shone out sidewise upon the water. Arnol took a step, his foot struck a stone, and he fell.

"What was that?"

The voice was one that he knew. He heard a step; some one emerged from the darkness, and stood holding a lantern high in air. Arnol lay like a mouse behind the shelter of his rock.

"Do you see anything?"

"Ah! I know that voice," said Arnol to himself. "It is the voice of the little black Spanish doctor."

"What should I see? It is your own imagining. We are cut off from shore; nothing can reach the cave."

Then Arnol knew where he was. It was the

island cave, near the ford, to which he had walked many a time, dry shod, when the river was low.

" This devil's river is rising, still."

" Yes, it is rising, still."

" For the love of the saints, what shall we do, then?" asked the doctor, anxiously. "The silver cannot be floated away, but we — we can be washed down to the sea."

The first voice took up the argument.

" If we find that it still rises, say at the end of a half hour, we must swim for it. We can always return for the silver. We can hide it at the back there under the loose rocks; no one will look there, — no, not for a thousand years! The ghost of the pirate is always roaming there."

" Leave it here! That for which we have risked so much! Not I! We have the padre's murder already on our souls; shall we lose that for which we have risked our own lives?"

Murder! What was this talk of murder? Arnol quaked as he lay there. Should they discover him, they would kill him, too, because he had spied upon them. Holy saints! would they never take away that lantern with its hateful, searching light!

" And I," said the little Spanish doctor, " I cannot swim."

"Then the padre's Mexican dollars need not be divided."

There was a quarrel, high words, a blow! and a form fell with a thud upon the beach. The slash of a machete to make sure. Then followed a dragging sound, and a quivering body went swirling away in the now boiling flood; and shortly a living being struck out for the shore, and Arnol was left alone upon the dreadful island.

The boy dragged his boat up as high as possible; then he climbed to the roof of the cave, and waited. Would the waters engulf him? should he be washed away to the sea, as helpless as the little Spanish doctor, or should he be saved? He watched the long night through, and when the day began to show in the east he descended to the beach. The river was still running furiously, but it was no higher, and the boat was there, just awash. Ah! that word murder, it hung heavy on his heart. The good padre murdered! He must hasten ashore, at no matter what risk, and tell the colonias all that he knew. And now a sudden doubt possessed the boy. Could he have dreamed it all? Was it some horrid, waking nightmare? He ran to the mouth of the cave. Ah, no! it was not a dream. There lay the great bags on the floor; some of the silver dollars had rolled out,

and lay strewn upon the ground. He urged his
boat into the water, and with a bound and a
push he was off. The Sangre de Cristi lilies,
which were so brilliant yesterday, now hung
limp and withered over the sides of the boat,
and trailed in the water like streaks of blood.
The craft whirled and swirled with dizzy speed,
but a beneficent eddy carried her toward the
bank. And though she struck upon a rock
and threw Arnol into the water, he clung to
the rock; and then, with a strong leap, was
ashore. He scrambled up the bank, and came
out just opposite the casa of Inez. No one was
awake. Arnol contented himself with rapping
upon the shutter near the head of Inez's bed, and
shouting, —

" I espit upon thee and thy great coward, Luis;
I espit upon thee and thy skate-fish child." He
listened; he heard Luis say to Inez: —

" What is that?"

He heard Inez answer, "It is the ghost of
the little Arnol; he has been drowned." But
Luis said in reply to her: —

"A ghost indeed! It is too late, I tell thee,
for ghosts. Has not the red cock crowed for
four o'clock? Look at the light creeping under
the thatch."

Then Arnol rapped louder, and Laura awoke
and normally cried.

" I espit upon thee, and thy coward Luis, and thy skate-fish child."

Arnol edged away down the path to the corner of the wood, and soon had the rickety gate between himself and the casa. He fastened the wire that locked the gate, and danced in the pathway like a sprite of evil. The door of the casa opened. Luis looked darkly out. Arnol danced and shouted derisively, the chorus of his song being, " I espit upon thee, oh, yes! thou, and thy lazy Inez, and thy skate-fish Laura." Luis's raiment was scanty, but there were no onlookers. When he started swiftly toward Arnol, the sprite turned and fled into the depths of the ceiba forest.

When Arnol entered the bodega, Plumero the Good was behind the counter weighing out some rice for an early customer. The good padre had just arisen. Pale was he, and his head was bound with a bandage. He walked weakly from the inner room as Arnol entered the door.

" And there is the little Arnol," he said, in his gentle voice. " The boy is down from the hills betimes! And what will the little Arnol have so early in the morning?"

Arnol screwed up his eyes and looked at Plumero the Good.

" Where is the little black Spanish doctor? " he asked.

Plumero started and grew pallid. He trembled so that the scales went all awry.

"Careful, Plumero! careful! See how my rice is being spilled, at least ten or twelve grains on the floor. Careful, I say."

The peon tipped up the scale so that his precious rice ran back to the level again.

"Look at him, padre."

"Thou imp of evil, and what wilt thou have with the doctor? He went back two nights ago to Puerto la Mar."

"By the water, Plumero? Ah, see him tremble, padre!"

The padre was dazed.

"What is that thou wilt have, child?"

"I'll have his life, padre!"

The good padre leaned against the counter.

"More talk of killing? His life? The life of Plumero the Good! I do not understand."

"First for killing you, padre, in the dark, and next for stealing your cockfighting dollars. The little Spanish doctor was not of much account, and will not be missed."

"My dollars! My dollars! Where are they? Oh, where, where?"

Plumero the Good was stealing toward the door.

"Go, if you like," said Arnol, scornfully. "The island is large, but you cannot escape."

Carlos Plumero entered the door at that moment.

"And it was my machete that was used," said Plumero the Bad, as he laid his hand on the shoulder of Plumero the Good.

"And as for your cockfighting dollars, padre, I will tell to no one but you and the Don Billyblake where they are at this moment."

The peons laid strong hands on the form of Plumero the Good. Cristoforo Colon sat up in his corner and raised a feeble crow. His dollars were found. Don Billy Blake had been leaning in at the doorway, thinking with unusual violence. He looked at Plumero as the peons tied his ankles together with a rope.

"I told you not to break the eleventh commandment," said Don Billy. "You wasn't willin' not to talk, you know."

PAUL'S ORANGE GROVE

PAUL'S ORANGE GROVE

Don César paused on his way to the river. He heard shouts of protestation, mingled with much good-natured laughter. What could it mean?

It was the peons' holiday. Don César's kindly nature made him hesitate to disturb them. He meditated. Shall I go back? Shall I go forward? Leaning out to a tree growing by the side of the path, from an air plant isolated upon its trunk, he plucked a gigantic red lily, a lily of many leaves. He began to pull them, and, as they dropped in the pool by the horse's feet, he whispered, "Forward, back, forward, back, forward." Ah! the pistils alone stood straight and yellow upon the stem. Forward it was.

The gray started. Don César raised his eyes.

Toward him, along the plastic way, advanced a stately caryatid, the first one ever seen in motion. Her noble head was poised with dignity upon a neck fit for a sculptor's model. Her beautiful arm — not darker than the traces a summer's sun might leave upon the cheek of a Northern belle — was upraised to hold in place a basket, where the freshly washed linen glistened in the still fierce, though declining, light of the sun. From the small ears depended large circles of gold, which scarce were moved by her tread, so slow and measured. The straight nose and brows, the firm lines of the mouth, showed force and strength. The curling lashes shaded the gray eyes to black. The glossy hair, blue in its lights, waved grandly back from the low brow, and twisted in a great coil behind the head, above the shapely neck. In the calm lines of this face there was no suggestion of annoyance. The flowing white muslin had escaped from its detaining pin, and was trailing through shallow pools, over wet sods, or catching now and again on a burr, or else was held in the persistent grasp of a thorny behucca.

But nothing either hastened or detained this dusky caryatid. She moved along on her stately way. The gown might tear or pull free as it listed; her pace did not vary.

"Oh, it's you, Sibyl! What is going on down at the river?"

A pleasant glance accompanied Don César's words.

"They bathe Emanuel, the Porto Ricanian; that is all, Señor." Sibyl permitted her lips to part in a dignified smile, which disclosed her handsome teeth.

"And why should they bathe Emanuel?"

"I have heard it said, Señor, that some of his race need much of the soap as well as of the water. The sand on the river bank is also of use. Buen' dia', Señor."

Sibyl passed on with stately step.

Don César sat looking after the vanishing form. And as he sat there he mused:—

"The native is cleanly as to his person, though I fear as much cannot be said for his morals. Now Sibyl there—" He paused, shook his head impatiently, and chirruped to the gray. "Why blame the native, when the white man sets the pace?" But the flower-fortune had sentenced him to go forward. A few yards of lively pacing brought him to the river bank.

The energetic peons were still rolling Emanuel in the stream. That river, which at times rises to the proportions of a turbulent flood, was to-day but a clear little brooklet, winding in and out among its stepping-stones and over its gravelly bed. It sang its smiling song in "little sharps and trebles," whose music fell upon unheeding ears. There was not depth enough for bathing in the shallow water, but the peons had found a small pool, and into this they had plunged the newcomer, Emanuel. As Don

César approached they ceased their efforts, and
one after the other turned to walk away ; all, in
fact, but Barron.   He had some standing in the
community and felt his importance not a little.

"And is that the way in which you treat the
stranger here in your own country?"   Don César
frowned, but his dark teeth would show a little.

"Como no, Don César?"   It was Barron who
spoke.   At this the others plucked up courage.
Did not Barron own the finest game-cock between Haldez and Castella, and what other
thing under the sun could give a man a better
standing, always excepting, of course, Pedro
Bolero's gambling-house?   The peons turned and
gazed questioningly at Don César.   Don César
had once seen a comic opera, when he visited
Madrid many years ago.   He was transported
back over the space of years.   He could almost
see the footlights and smell the flowers.   The
men formed an irregular line, and, looking for
support to Barron, they broke into a chorus of
"Como no, Don César?   Como no, como no?
Como no, Don César?   Como no?"

Then Barron took up the solo, while the
picturesque peons assumed attentive attitudes
and waited for their chance at the chorus.
Barron gesticulated as he spoke : —

"We of our country are of the clean ones ;
he of his country is of the soiled ones.   We will

not wash beside him, we will not eat beside him.
Why not cleanse him in the little water that
the Rio Frio still leaves to us?"

"Ah, I see! the greatest good to the greatest
number, Barron."

Recitative: "Then why not cleanse him, Don
César?"

Chorus: "Como no, Don César? Como no,
como no, como no, Don César? Como no?"

"But you are mistaken, Barron. You are
ignorant; you have not travelled." Consterna-
tion and amazement depicted on the faces of the
chorus. Barron ignorant! What would they
hear next? "I have been in his island. They
are a cleanly people. You must not judge all
his race by one specimen."

There were sounds of horse's hoofs upon the
opposite bank. Barron, somewhat abashed,
turned away. The downcast chorus followed
him up the slope. A horseman emerged from
the wood across the river. He came from the
direction of Puerto la Mar. He cantered his
horse down to the sand cove and spurred him
into the water. The tired animal bent his head
and let his curling lips rest daintily upon the
surface of the shining pool. He seemed to be
drinking in liquid blue and pink and gold, for
the sun was getting low; its level light made of
the surface of the water a symphony of color.

"Bastante! bastante!" said the rider, as he felt the sides of his horse swell between his legs. He jerked impatiently at the bridle; the beast raised his head high in air, his moving lips dripping diamonds. A touch of the spur started him splashing across the ford to where Don César sat. "Ah! it is you, Don César!" said the young man. "What is all this commotion?"

"They have been washing the new man, Enrique. You know that the peons will not tolerate an uncleanly person among them."

Don César spoke in French because he was Spanish; the newcomer spoke in Spanish because he was French. Neither one could be said to speak with fluency, but what would you have? One must preserve his manners even though his morals go by the board.

"I know, I know!" Henri de Silva laughed heartily as he surveyed the wretched Emanuel who was struggling to stretch his damp shirt over a wet and swollen back. "Our people are more cleanly on the exterior than they are interiorly."

"The outside of the cup and platter, literally," chimed in the older man; "but, my boy, are we any better?"

Don Enrique seemed willing to change the subject. He sat looking up the river course.

"I have always thought the Rio Frio, at this

time of year, an excellent place in which to dry clothes," he said.

"You would have changed that opinion, Enrique, could you have seen Sibyl just now. She was walking up to La Primavera, her basket full to the top with wet linen."

Don César glanced obliquely at de Silva as he spoke. The other turned abruptly and said, with a gesture of impatience : —

"How weary one gets of it all!" He lapsed into his native French. "Why did they send me here, I wonder? I was a boy when I came. How one ages in such a place! Ten years in this God-forsaken hell!"

Don César laughed good-naturedly.

"You are extreme to-day, my boy. There are times when you do not find it so bad. Why did you not go to Hayti? There you would have heard your mother tongue at least. You would have known — "

"I should probably have known 'battle and murder and sudden death,' as the English book of prayers puts it. I looked over it with the English consul's young daughter when I was last at 'The City.' Ah! there is a girl for example! Non merci! No Hayti for me!" Don Enrique flicked the dust from his high gaiters. "Strange! the roads are muddy, but the high grass retains the dust so long!"

T

"It was a sudden shower, shortly over," said
Don César. "It shows only in the paths."

"There is, however, one gleam of hope," continued Don Enrique. He did not look at Don
César as he spoke. "That same English girl, she
comes to-morrow, perhaps to-day. She is sister
to the wife of Talbot, he who lives at Primavera. Ah! she is charming!" De Silva drew
a long sigh. "She is good. She would make
something of a man; she would arouse energy
in any one. She is the one pure thing in this
vile land. She will be a godsend." He added
emphatically, though under his breath, "Dieu
Donnée!"

"Take care, Enrique; do not get entangled
there."

"Pourquoi pas?"

Don César was silent. The friends turned
their horses and mounted the river bank. The
peons had gone on before them. Emanuel the
Purified was sulkily struggling with his damp
clothing. The riders had not noticed his presence, though he had been close at their horses'
heels. He passed them by with a surly nod as
they mounted the slope, his black skin almost
red from the unusual manipulation to which it
had been subjected.

"That's the man who follows my Sibyl everywhere," said de Silva.

" Your Sibyl ? "

" Well, well, Don César! you know very well what I mean. My housekeeper, Sibyl."

" She is a very beautiful woman, Enrique, — girl, rather ; she is little more than a girl."

" She is well enough, Don César."   De Silva spoke impatiently.   " I have often wondered why that tree which stands out so far in the river, you know the one I mean, the gri-gri on the point of land just above the ford, why it has not been swept away in some flood."

" That is a monarch, Enrique, but it will go some day. The land on which it stands is rather high, as you know. Its roots must strike deep. I have always thought that the river course must have changed, encroached rather above and below that point; or else it has taken a sudden sweep below. That tree stands, I should think, about the middle of the river, even with the middle of the ford."

" A strange river it is, and it has many re- markable things about it; that large rock below the ford, for instance. Did you ever notice the hole that the water has bored directly through it ? "

Don César saw that de Silva was talking simply for the sake of tabooing one vexed subject.

" Enrique, my boy, you will bore a hole through me if you dwell any longer on that

wretched river.   Come and look at my new
cacao drying-house."

They dismounted, and tied their horses to
branches in the grateful shade.   Don César unlocked the door of the drying-house.   With
much apparent pride he showed to de Silva the
arrangement of the interior.   He pushed the
drying-car out of the house and in again, to
prove how little force was required to move a
load of fresh seeds into the sun, or to return
them to shelter for the night, or during a storm
of rain.   De Silva must examine the padlock,
fastened securely by what Don César called a
" Yaleock."   He said this over and over, " my
yaleock," "this yaleock," " that yaleock," until
de Silva had become as tired of Don César's conversation as Don César had of his.   As each one
grew more weary of the other, he waxed more
polite.

Meanwhile Sibyl moved on her stately way.
Her steady walk had brought her to the path
which runs through the palm grove just below
the colonia of La Primavera.   The sun's rays
were still scorching.   Haste was unnecessary,
foolish; there was an occasional patch of deep
shade.   The basket of wet linen protected her
head.   Sometimes she halted and rested, leaning,
tall and straight, against a shaft no more erect
than she.   As she stood thus she was aware of the

patter of quick feet thumping soft in the elastic clay, left moist by the afternoon shower. Sibyl's curiosity was not aroused. Perhaps that element of her composition had never been developed. She had rested, and it was time to start again; a few steps brought her to a fallen tree of gigantic proportions which lay directly across the path. She was within the colonia of La Primavera now. Its master had contracted many native habits. That tree might lie there a century, might crumble and rot piecemeal, before an axe would be laid to its grand bulk. Sibyl placed one slippered foot upon a sturdy branch, the other upon a bole, and so by slow steps she mounted, her splendid height showing at its best as she stood for a moment upon the curve of the rough bark flooring. Then she descended as regally as she had mounted. Her path regained, she moved on.

A leap, a bound, and Emanuel was beside her. His eyes were angry, his body glowed with its enforced though cleanly punishment. Little streams from his forehead watered the ground. His shirt, stained with banana juice, clung damply to his shoulders. His red and white checked belt was empty, for he swung his machete in his hand as he ran breathless along the path.

"You go to La Primavera?" he asked.

" Como no, hombre ? "

The caryatid did not turn her head. Emanuel had only a view of the clear-cut classic profile.

" You have the washing for the Señora at La Primavera ? "

" Como no, hombre ? "

" You do not bring it finished, only washed ? "

" Como no, hombre ? "

" You will wash willingly for the white Señorita, when she arrives ? "

" Como no, hombre ? "

The voice was steady ; but there was a tremor of the eyelid, a twitching round the muscle of the nostril.

" That white Señorita, she is of the Don Enrique's class, not of *yours — and — mine.*" Emanuel paused before the utterance of the last three words; he emphasized them. Sibyl walked on, silent. A breeze came down from the hill and blew her white gown outward. It flowed toward the edges of the path ; it touched Emanuel as he paced beside her. " I have listened to the conversation of the Don Enrique."

" Como no, hombre ? " Sibyl could not resist breaking through the monotony of her usual reply. " That does not surprise me," she said ; " worms like you always listen."

"Worm or not, I have heard that which will not please you."

"Porque, hombre?"

"This affectation of the Spanish tongue does not please me; it angers me."

"Porque, hombre?"

"You can easily understand if you will. A white Señorita comes to La Primavera to-morrow perhaps, perhaps to-day."

"Como no, hombre?"

"If you know not, I know not; if you know, I know, and know you do, and know I do. Is it necessary that I reveal to you her name?"

Sibyl did not turn her head; apparently she was not interested in Emanuel's revelations.

"Do you remember the reward that the Señor Don Enrique promised to any one who should find a packet he had lost in the woods? You remember that he lost it on his way up from the mail station at Caño Sandros. He promised, as you know, five Mexican dollars to him who should find the parcel. Five good Mexican dollars, fresh from the bank at Puerto la Mar. Very well, then! It was I who found that packet. It had lain in the woods for some days. The edges of the paper were soaked by the rain. I was looking at it, not too curiously; I did pull the edges a trifle, certainly, and the hard round thing slipped out in my hand. The spring opened but too willingly. I had to give it but little aid. As I stood there in the depths of the ceiba forest, a young white girl looked up at me. A young white girl, do you hear?"

"Ha! A spy as well as a listener!" Sibyl could not resist that much.

"And I can say to you this, you with your 'Como no,' and 'Como no,' that if I am a worm, that such worms have keen ears. Oh, yes! ears that understand all things. Shall I tell you who I heard say this very hour — down there by the drying-house — that the coming of this beautiful young white" — Emanuel laid stress upon the adjective — "Señorita would be a send of the good God?"

Sibyl drew in her breath, and compressed her straight lips.

"Como no, hombre?"

"Who but the Don Enrique! Don Enrique de Silva, who lives at El Monte. Now you have it. Don Enrique, our Don Enrique, your Don Enrique."

"And why should he not speak of whom he wills?" The usually calm voice trembled somewhat. "Why should a carrion of a pig from San Juan de Porto Rico make his remarks upon what the Señor Don Enrique de Silva chooses to do or to say? What is it then to a beast of a stranger, who must be washed by the cleanly

natives before he is fit for their company,
whether a young white Señorita comes or does
not come to-day or to-morrow, to visit her family
at La Primavera? Do you think that I am
blind and deaf, because I am dumb? And who
are you that you should break the silence? If
the good God gave us always justice, he would
stiffen your vile tongue so that it could not pour
out your treacherous thoughts. In what way
does it concern any of us that the Señor Don
William Talbotte has invited the Señora's young
sister to inhabit his casa for a while? He can
have whom he wishes at La Primavera, I suppose; the place is his own. Did you think that
he must ask us? Can you prevent it, pig of a
Porto Ricanian, or can I help it if I would?
Blacks that we are and always must remain!"

Sibyl dwelt upon the objectionable word with
bitter emphasis. Those few almost unperceiv-
able dark drops in her veins, got, she knew not
where or how, had shut her out from the tradi-
tions of her actual race, and from equality with
it — a race to which by manner, appearance, and
speech she belonged. For Sibyl had grasped at
all that seemed to her best in her limited surroundings. Opportunity given, what possibilities
were hers! She saw on every side mixed mar-
riages, resulting sometimes from interwoven
lives such as her own. Had no wedge come to

part them, who knows what might have been! Perhaps it was not too late. Perhaps this horror was not to be. Her world had held for her but one love, but one faith. If she lost this!— She had forgotten Emanuel at her side.

"It is of your choice to name me carrion of a pig, but I shall have your thanks when I spy out the land at Primavera and bring you word what goes on there. Don Enrique is fire and tow all in one, as they say in old Spain. I heard him say but now that he was weary of it all. Does that mean you, Sibyl? you?"

The woman, with hand still raised to steady her basket, stopped short in her two soft imprints. She turned her supple body from the hips. Compressing her lips and making a hollow of her cheeks, she opened her mouth a slit only, and spat at Emanuel straight between the eyes. Then without a word she turned again to the front, placed one slippered foot before the other, and moved statuesquely onward. Sibyl saw a swift shadow fly like a bird across the sunlit path. It was Emanuel's machete raised threateningly above his head. She did not shrink; they were in full sight of the casa now, and Emanuel was a coward.

At La Primavera all was excitement. Yellow old Lores, toothless and wizened, was putting fresh curtains at the windows. These the

Señora Talbot would have, regardless of the Señor's insistence that they provided fine hiding-places for black spiders.[1] The veranda was being washed, and a deluge poured down the broad front steps.

"Not so much water, Pete, for the love of the saints! Not so much water!" Lores called from the paneless opening. "Must I tell you a hundred times that we have but five barrels left? and unless we get some heavy rain, the good God alone knows what we shall do! What with the Señor with his English ways, taking his tub every morning, and with the Señora washing William the Orange One as if he were human, we shall soon have not a drop. Why dogs cannot be washed in the river passes my comprehension.

"And to name an animal after a grand gentleman like our Don William!" When Lores began to grumble, even her adored mistress came in for a share. "She thinks it a fine piece of wit, our Señora, because the wretched dog is yellow, the color of an orange, to call him some foolish name. There are people like that; very sensible ones, the good God knows. She will tell you with all seriousness — oh, yes, with all seriousness — that the Orange One is the king of dogs. She will tell you with all

[1] Tarantulas.

seriousness that she has named him after two
kings; do you hear? two kings! The Señor
Don William, and another king in the history
books. *Another king!* Thou good God! It
is the Señora indeed who has the humor!

"And then there is the cooking. Oh, but the
cooking! The red beans must be well boiled,
or they would stick in our stomachs forever;
and to the sin coche you must add water once
and again; and look, will you, how much goes
off in steam!" Lores's cavern of a mouth was
filled with tacks, and her monologue was not
always easy to understand.

"Ah! There is Sibyl from El Monte. It is
more than well that she can wash in the river
these days; otherwise what should we do? Go
round to the wash-house, Sibyl; Maria will take
the clothes and iron them, please God, in time
for the coming Sunday, for are we not all to
attend the cockfight at the Padre Martinez's
bodega? That priest has a fine cock, but not
so fine a one as that of the young schoolmaster.
I have put my month's wages on him; twenty
good Mexican dollars. He possesses the cock
now these three months. He is the red and
yellow cock which belonged to the old Alcalde
at Haldez."

This Ollendorfian sentence was cut short by a
cough and a choke. A tack had slipped down,

and was stranded across the ever-full windpipe of
Lores.   One may feel grateful, even to a tack.

Sibyl walked round the house, and set her
basket down at the door of the wash-room.   A
centipede ran across the door-sill.   Maria caught
up the ever-ready machete, and divided the
many-legged horror into several pieces.   William the Orange One ran close, barking and
nosing at the wriggling divisions.   He caught
them, and tossed them in air.   The cat, St.
Michael, pawed and worried at things fast be-
coming inanimate.   Sibyl stood and watched
Maria, as she put the finishing touch to a dainty
white spread that she had been pressing.   She
scorned to ask a question.   Emanuel thrust his
dark head in at the doorway.

   " You will have the company ? "

   " You ain' yere ?   Don William an' de Señora
gone fer to meet her."

   Emanuel looked at Sibyl, watching her, as he
asked,

   " Her ?   Who ? "

   "You ain' done yere?   Comp'ny ain' so mighty
common in dese yer pa'ts.   Seems like a year
since de ol' Moddom leff."   Maria leaned over
and let her weight rest heavily upon the iron,
thus pressing a crease down the middle of her
spread.   She spoke in jerks, from a region below
her diaphragm.   " You ain' done yere !   My,

my! Why, it's de young Señorita, 'Manuel, f'om
De City.   Our Señora's brudda, Don Andrea,
counsul dere.   Ain' you know dat?"

Emanuel watched Sibyl in silence.

"Emanuel, thou lazy one, come and help Pete
to remove this empty barrel.   Empty!   Thou
good God!"

Emanuel gone, Sibyl spoke.

"Did not the Señora Talbotte once show me
her portrait, Maria?"

"Isposo," Maria answered, in one word.
"Mo'n likely.   Stands in dere on de piany forty;
mighty laikely lukin' young lady; had de calentura at De City; comin' yere fo' a change; reckon
all de gen'l'men folks be a-shootin' each odder
fo' her favors."   Maria belonged to that colony
at Saltona which had migrated long ago from
the American slave states.   The language has
changed little in all these years.

Sibyl passed through the wash-room door, and
into the kitchen.   Old Gomez was watching the
sin coche as it bubbled and steamed over the hot
fire.   He was perspiring freely, the doors were
all open.   Sibyl stepped with a long stride over
the little girl who was peeling green yams in the
doorway.   She descended the two steps, and
crossed the side yard to the veranda.

"Come not here!" screamed Lores, who, to
the discomfiture of the listeners, had coughed up

the beneficent tack. "Come not here. I wish no mud from the river tracked over my clean veranda."

Sibyl stopped half-way up the steps.

"I will not offend you by entering, Lores. I ask only that you will show to me the portrait of the young Señorita who will arrive to-day or to-morrow from Caño Sandros."

Peter joined in with his share of inhospitable warning.

"Don' move, fo' de Lawd's sake! dirtyin' up my clean veranda. Shoo! Keep dem chickens off, Sibyl. I's fairly 'stracted. Lores's gab set me jus' wild! De picsure, you say? I'll git it, Sibyl. Oh, I ain' talkin' to you, Lores! I git it, Sibyl, ef you on'y stan' still. Now, don' you move, fo' de Lawd's sake!"

"I have no wish to enter, Peter, if you will only show me the portrait."

They were beautiful, serious eyes that looked at Sibyl from out the silver frame. Yes; it was the same. She had seen its counterpart in the blue velvet case which Don Enrique kept locked away from all eyes save his own. But men are careless, even when they think themselves most careful. In that island climate, clothing is constantly changed; keys are left in pockets, and Sibyl had some rights. It was not mere curiosity that had induced Sibyl to seek for the portrait when Don Enrique had left El Monte. It was a deep and anxious feeling of interest in what she was beginning to fear might result in something of a tragic nature to herself.

"Any one would love her." Sibyl sighed as she said these words. She laid the picture back on Lores's dust-cloth, and descended the steps. She was half-way through the palm grove when Gomez caught her, — breathless.

"Youah basket, Sibyl; youah done fo'got."

"I remember nothing these days, it seems to me; the basket could easily have waited until I returned for it."

"P'haps dat's what you figgerin' fo'. Eveybody plannin' to see de young Señorita."

"No; I shall come no more to La Primavera. Buen' noch', Gomez." Sibyl turned away with a dissatisfied shrug of the shoulders. "Gomez was always forward," she muttered half aloud.

With a graceful swing of the arm, she placed the light basket upon her head and continued her homeward progress. She had remained over time at La Primavera, and though her passage through the palm grove was attended by a glimmering light, she saw, when she entered the mompoia growth, that the night was deepening fast. She had walked for a quarter hour, when the tramp of a horse's hoofs sounded near; they came from the opposite direction. Sibyl stepped to the side of the path, and stood in the shadow of the trees. Don César came into view; he did not see Sibyl until the gray snorted and shied.

"Oh! it's you, Sibyl; you really frightened me, standing there so ghostly. It's the second time to-day that you have caused El Cid to start. Buenas noches." He was passing on.

"Has Don Enrique returned to El Monte, Señor?"

Don César reined in his horse.

"Oh, yes, a half hour ago; why?"

"I — I — thought that he might have gone to Caño Sandros, Señor."

"And why?"

"He — he — is talking of buying a new bull from the big company. Buen' noch', Señor!"

"Buenas noches, Sibyl! or stay; shall I accompany you back to the bridge?"

"I would not trouble the Señor; I am not afraid."

"Don't loiter on the way, then. Buenas noches!"

The night grew darker. The red glow which had illumined the tree trunks when first she entered the wood had faded to a cold gray. It betokened the quick fall of night. A mocking-bird, whose variety of trills had been sounding in Sibyl's ear all the way from La Primavera, ceased his song. He had found his nest. The

U

parrots screamed no more; they had gone home
for the night.   The cooing dove mournfully
called in the depths of the sombre wood; and
once a great owl, with staring eyes, shrieked
loudly in Sibyl's ears.   A pair of bats flew cir-
cling round and brushed her hair in their flight.
Sibyl's heart fluttered in her throat.   Supersti-
tion was her inheritance, and the woods were
full of mystery.

Should she see him then, that headless male-
factor?   Was he waiting for her down below
there, lurking beneath the shadow of the mompoia trees, his fleshless head held in glistening,
bony fingers, lights streaming from his eyeless
sockets?   She must sing; he could not harm
her then.   Her heart was thumping loudly.
The blood pulsed against her ears, her knees
threatened to let her fall in the black and lonely
path; but she must sing.   Her magnificent con-
tralto voice rose tremulous upon the night air.
She poured forth the incantatory chant of the
night-wandering peon; she repeated it, and yet
again, gaining courage with repetition.   The
cacao leaves rustled; a cacao pod fell to the
ground; following suit, a mamey apple, over-
ripe to retain its hold, thumped deep into the
sodden leaves.   The banana fringes courtesied
and swayed toward each other, waving square-
cut fingers now up, now down.   Whispers ran

up through the tall, central scrolls, saying to the
older leaves, "Unwind, unwind! for we are new
and fresh and young, and would take your places."

Little tremors shook the behuccas from ground
to branch fifty feet overhead, and agitated the
gigantic leaves which bent over fan-like at the
junction of vine and tree; numberless unac-
countable noises filled the air, for Nature busy
with her Master's orders could be heard now that
daily animal motion was stilled, and Sibyl's nervous ear was strained to catch the most evanescent sound.   It rose again! her song — more
beautiful for fear.   Ah! how dark it was down
there in the bottom!   A white mist was creeping
up from the river, and the moon had not yet
risen.   The scent of flowers pressed down upon
the air, heavy, sickening; it could almost be felt.
Would no one hear her sing? would no one come
to meet her?   Did no one now care that she was
abroad so late, alone?   Time was — ah! there
was the rise; she was near home now.   Why
was all so dark?   She looked eagerly upward.
There! see! a tiny light gleamed forth.   Some
one was lighting the veranda lantern, which hung
there as a guide to the traveller belated.   Now
it shone, a thread of gold through the mist,
streaming down the hillside!   She caught the
sound of the stamping of hoofs upon the stable
floor, and men's cheerful voices and laughter rang

out.   No need now to try to keep her courage
up ; but sing she would, for there was one little
heart to listen and be glad.   Ah ! this was home.
Her home ! the only place on the earth that she
loved — that palm-board square, with yagua
thatch covering its many irregularities of roof.
She gained the crest of the hill ; a flood of light
poured from the open doorway.   A little boy,
pale of color, fair of hair, stood there eagerly
scanning the impenetrable darkness.

"Madre ! " he called, with questioning cry.
He bounded down the steps, his straw slippers
patting the earth.

"Paul, my little Paul ! "   She took him in her
arms and held him close.

A month passed by — a month of long weary
days to those who were anxious and sick at
heart, a month of fleeting delicious days to those
whose waking thoughts were bliss, whose dreams
were heaven.   It was a month full of pleasant
warmth.   It brought breezes, soft to the cheek
as a thistledown's caress ; it brought languorous
scents from leaf and flower.   Its every day
brought to Sibyl a waking to heavy and dread
surmises, to de Silva with each hour some new
phase of pleasure.   He was always at La Primavera, and the serious gray eyes watched for
his happy coming.

Sibyl still carried her linen to the river.   She

was anxious, nervous; she made work for her-self; her busy hands were never still; and when he had left El Monte, she never failed to search for the key of that carefully locked drawer, and, when she had found it, take from its hiding-place the velvet case, and look long and ear-nestly into those eyes which answered back her gaze with so cold a regard.

It was a month since Sibyl had returned from La Primavera. The Señora had sent for her some-times, but she had always been too busy to respond.

Emanuel mounted the slope leading up to the Casa of El Monte one early morning. The fog was abroad over all the valley. Only the tree-tops upon the different elevations caught the eye like green oases in a sea of white. Emanuel's head peered up out of the mist, then his shadowy form came into view; then a man of flesh and blood left the wall of mystery behind him, and stood tall and lean by the lattice-work between the pilotillos. Sibyl sat upon the topmost step, her chin resting in her upturned palm, her eyes gazing across the green islands in their milky lake. She saw nothing. Emanuel stood for a moment regarding her; she did not turn her head or speak to him.

" Where is Don Enrique ? " asked Emanuel. Getting no reply, he repeated the words. " Where is Don Enrique ? "

"What is that to you?"

Sibyl turned upon him coldly. Such rev-
eries as hers might well be disturbed, but she
would have preferred to choose the cause and
the disturber. Emanuel was gaunt and lean;
his haggard eyes had a hungry look as he bent
them upon the woman. He too possessed an
inheritance of blood and tradition which was
on a plane far above his surroundings.

"I did not expect an answer; I can answer
for myself. He is at La Primavera. He did
not return last night."

A violent rain began to fall while Emanuel
was speaking. The mist began to fade away,
for a wind was sweeping down from the mountains and, like a pair of strong hands, was rolling
the thick white blanket over and over, leaving
the valley bare and green behind. Emanuel's
voice had for accompaniment the scattering patter of great drops of silver; molten bullets they
seemed, as they dropped upon the broad fan-
like banana leaves and bounded thence to the
ground.

"And has he not the right to remain away if
he will? Who controls him?"

"No one, *now!*"

Sibyl rose; she stood, tall and splendid, looking down upon Emanuel. She drew a long, sob-
bing sigh. The anger that she would have

shown a month ago did not rise within her at
her bidding. She moistened her dry lips with
as dry a tongue; she felt weary. Emanuel's
words seemed to have fallen upon a partly
paralyzed ear. One who could understand the
working of a nature like hers would have said,
perhaps, that her spirit was broken. She turned,
and walked toward the doorway.

"Listen, Sibyl!"

"I will not listen! Go your way!" The tone
was not an angry one. She stated her decision
in a monotonous voice, which had in it not a
trace of feeling; she was so weary of it all.

"Oh, listen!" Emanuel stretched out his
bony hands. "Oh, listen! Sibyl! I beg of
you, listen! If this man, this Don Enrique,
were not longer in the world, would you —"

"Begone, Emanuel! Begone, I say!" The
words conveyed a certain meaning, but Sibyl's
tone contained neither emphasis or expression.
She sighed again, as if tired of the effort of
speaking. "If you do not go, I shall call
Roberto and Anastasio to put you again in
the river."

"I care not for Roberto! I care not for
Anastasio!" Emanuel's tones were full of passion and feeling. "I think that I am mad,
Sibyl. Oh! tell me, — I ask you, — if this
man, this Don Enrique —"

But Sibyl had dragged her languid steps into the room, and had closed the door.

The wind arose in swift gusts; the rain beat down. The new part of the house was roofed with corrugated zinc, whose flutings carried the precious water to the gutters just below the eaves. These were filled, at once, to overflowing. The flood, rushing along to the improvised conduit, — the half-section of a hollow trunk, — carried the water to the barrels standing at the corner of the veranda. Sibyl sat down by the open window. The lightning was abroad, now. She heard mutterings of thunder and, nearer than that, another rumbling. It was the stablemen rolling heavy casks along the veranda's length, to catch all that was possible of what might prove to be an evanescent downpour. She heard Paul's childish laugh as he pretended to help the peons at their work.

A tearing, ripping crash, accompanied by a blinding glare! Forgetful, for a moment, of her misery, Sibyl raised her eyes toward the hill. A great tree had been rent half the length of its trunk, and its top swayed helplessly across the mountain path. The bark was torn in strips; great bands of glistening wood, wet with sap, were bent like cotton cloth. Her heart stood still. Suppose that he were out in the storm! Perhaps he was coming home, even now; home, perhaps, to her. There was a sound at the open shutter. Could it be! A throb of the heart! Suddenly, she was alive again; he was there! all was to be as before! A great joy irradiated her face; she turned, —

"Do you know that he is to marry, to-morrow? Do you know that all things are preparing, to-day, at Haldez? Do you know that the school-children are to sing? Do you know that all the choicest orange blossoms at El Monte are to be cut in the late afternoon, to strew before the bride?

She reached out her hand, and seized the hasp of the shutter. She slammed it fiercely to, and fastened it. The room was dark now, except for the light which crept in under the broad spaces beneath the eaves. She was dazed; she could not understand. "The — the — blossoms — from the orange grove — our orange grove! That grove which we planted together — Paul's orange grove. The grove which he said was to be little Paul's fortune. The blossoms from Paul's orange grove! Paul's orange grove!" Over and over ran the words; through her tired brain they whirled with sickening monotony. Paul's orange grove! Oh, no! it could not be! He would not hurt her so. She saw as plainly as if they were present in the darkened room, the serious eyes, the calm face, the chestnut hair;

and wreathed through its wavy tendrils, Paul's flowers.

Sibyl sat there until the late afternoon. And then, the rain having ceased, mechanically she took up her basket of linen, and walked down the hill toward the river. Arrived at the bank, she descended the path which ran parallel with the flow of the water. Upon the flat stone, at the river's edge, she placed her basket. When first she reached the stone the water was far below her. She had to lean down to rinse the linen.

After she had been there for a while, there fell upon her ear a sawing, grating sound. She pushed aside the branches, and peered across the stream. All was deserted there. She then climbed the steep bank behind her. Reaching the top, she took a few steps nearer the path and, standing in the concealment of a vine-clad trunk, she scrutinized the vista on either side; but she could not place the sound. Sibyl then came out into the path, crossed it, and still screened by the foliage, she thrust her head through the branches toward the newly cleared potrero. This time she was more fortunate. Not a hundred yards away, a man was bending over the fence which enclosed the pasture. It was Emanuel. He was busy at the wire lately stretched from certain corner-posts that the cattle might not wander away. He was filing through the metal; Sibyl watched him, herself unseen.

Emanuel filed patiently on in the forest loneliness. Occasionally he turned his head, with a watchful air, to make sure that he was not observed. Once or twice he stopped and went to the edge of the bank and looked in the direction of the ford. Seeing no one, he returned and recommenced his patient work. At such times Sibyl shrank close to the ground, fearful that he would discover her presence. When Emanuel had cut the wire quite through, he paced a hundred feet along the side of the enclosure, and began to file afresh at the spot where he halted. Sibyl watched patiently. Don Enrique's interests for so long a time had been her own, that this spying upon an enemy was as second nature to her.

When Emanuel had cut the wire of the length that he desired, he coiled it into a ring, and started for the descent to the ford. The wire partly unwound, and trailed its length behind, catching in behuccas and vines; but Emanuel drew it after him, and, entering the hollow of a great tree, whose roots formed a chamber for concealment, he wound the loose end round the circle which he had made, and hid the whole away, quite out of sight. Then he descended the path to the ford and looked critically at the river, nodded his head as if well satisfied with what he saw, and, turning, mounted the hill and was swallowed up by the forest.

Sibyl stood regarding him as he vanished in the perspective of meeting branches. She stood with her hands on her hips, her handsome head bent a little to one side, her eyes almost closed, as if thus she could keep the thief longer within sight.

"The cep' for you to-morrow," she said aloud. "The cep', before you have had time to steal the rest. You have hidden it there that you may take it across the river and hide it in the old Demarisi rancho. But I have caught you! The cep' for you to-morrow."

To-morrow! Oh, to-morrow! If Emanuel had spoken truly, what matter who died or who lived, who was punished or who rewarded? To-morrow! to-morrow! He would even cut the blossoms from Paul's orange grove! Sibyl descended the bank again and raised her basket. One of the pieces had fallen upon the stone, and a yellow stain had marred its whiteness. She leaned over the water to rinse it again. What was this? She had not to lean so far. The river had risen; yes, surely it had risen! Well, what of that? And then swept through her being a pang of joy, — a pang akin to pain, so sharp and fierce was it. To-morrow! to-morrow! The river would be a rolling, dangerous flood by

to-morrow. The wedding-party could not cross
to Haldez; no, not to-morrow, not for many
days to come, perhaps. Who knew what might
happen before the water subsided? This was a
reprieve. The sudden change from utter dejec-
tion to hope dazed her. She stood looking down
upon the water below, running ever swifter
toward the lowlands and the sea. A smile was
upon her face. Yes, it must be so; the river
was rising! She looked across to the opposite
bank. The little pebble island was growing
smaller; the water had encroached upon it.

Little Paul met her half-way down the hill.
She kissed him with a fierce pressure that hurt
the child.

"Not to-morrow!" she whispered; "not to-
morrow!" And if not to-morrow, perhaps
never. Who could tell? The child gazed up at
her, wonderingly. Her mood was new to him.

When the light began to fade, Emanuel returned to the river. He went to the hollow
tree and drew forth the stolen coil of wire. He
peered across the stream, as well as up and
down, to assure himself of his entire isolation.
Seeing no one, he waded out to the middle of
the ford. He knew his path well; and, though
the water pushed strongly against his legs, he
kept a steady foothold. Was he not forced to
cross the ford every day when he went to cut

branches at the great company's cacao plantation? Who knew the path better than he?

Arrived at mid-stream, Emanuel turned and
walked up the river. The flow of the water was
hard to resist; its force was increasing. At last
he reached the large tree upon the projecting
point of land. He wound the end of his wire
round the trunk, and, bringing it back, twisted it
firmly round the original strand. With the
pincers that he held, he bent the wire in his
strong grasp like thread. There was a sudden
shout. Emanuel dropped the wire. He stood
erect and looked toward the sand cove. There,
through the fast-gathering dusk, he saw a man on
horseback. He recognized Don César.

"Is the water rising? Who is that? Oh!
You, Emanuel? I ask you, is the water rising?"

"Si, Señor; it will be a flood by midnight."

"What are you doing there?"

"Seeking my machete, which I lost yesterday."

Don César struck spurs to the sides of the
gray; they advanced into the stream.

"You must have wandered out of the path,
Emanuel."

Don César's voice sounded very faint, the
noise of the rushing water had become so loud.

"The river bed was nearly dry yesterday,
Señor; I was cutting up the old flat-boat which
stranded here a month ago."

"Ah, yes! Well! do not remain too late. Buenas noches, Emanuel."

"Buen' noch', Señor," said Emanuel, "and not any too soon," he added; this time without shouting.

The gray's hoofs rang out upon the landing-stone, and he and his master took their hurried way to "La Floresta."

When Don César had disappeared, Emanuel gathered up the coil, and carried it down stream and across the line of the ford. Haste was in every movement; he must finish quickly and leave the spot. Arrived at the rock below the ford, he forced the remaining end of his wire through the central hole of which de Silva and Don César had spoken, and clamped it as he had the upper end. He then waded with difficulty to the bank and waited.

The moon had just silvered the crest of the mountain when Don Enrique clattered up the slope of El Monte.

"He is coming! he is coming! coming home!" beat in the heart of one who was waiting.

"Quick, Roberto! you have not a moment to lose! Mount El Capitan, and take the baskets of orange blossoms to the church at Haldez. The river is rising fast. If we do not cross to-night, it may be many days before we can cross. Tell the padre that we are not a half

hour behind you. After you have left the baskets, ride to the coast and say that we shall take
the steamer to-morrow for ' The City.'   Hasten,
Roberto ; and remember to look after things
well while I am away."

The master of El Monte entered the casa,
threw down his hat, flung his belt upon the
floor, and took a change of linen from the ward-
robe.

" My boots, Francisco," he called ; " the long
ones, the riding-boots ; the river is higher than
I thought."

When the impatient bridegroom emerged
from the door of his room booted and spurred,
handsome, and impatient to be gone, the fresh
black horse was neighing at the foot of the
steps.   His spurs rang a joyous note, as he
hurriedly crossed the veranda.   As he reached
the landing, a tall figure arose from out the darkness and a hand was laid upon his.

" It is true, then ! you are going ! going to-
night ? "

Don Enrique bit his lip.

" You, Sibyl !   I thought that you had gone
to the upper farm.   They told me so.   Yes, I
go to-night."

" You will never be so mad !   The river is
running wild !   It will be certain death.   You
must not cross to-night."

" Such words will not stop me, Sibyl. I can still cross."

She held his hand more closely; she turned away her head.

" And Paul's orange trees?"

" Paul's — ? Oh, *that!* I will provide for the boy, Sibyl. Let me pass, let me pass, I say! The river rises every moment."

" When do you return?"

" Cease your questioning — let me pass! Do you not hear me say that the river rises?"

" Then all that has been is as nothing to you?"

" Don't be a fool, Sibyl! I tell you that I shall provide for you. There is no use in trying to awaken a dead past. I tell you that I must go, and at once!"

She put her hand behind her, and drew the wondering boy from the shadow of her form. She pushed him toward de Silva.

" And is this nothing?"

A second time he bit his lip; then he stooped and kissed the child.

" Little Paul, I shall not forget you," he said, and ran down the steps.

" And what of me?"

She leaned over the flower boxes just above his head. The jasmine vine encircled her grand beauty. The languorous scent of the flowers,

x

the flooding light of the moon, all that she had been to him, were blended inextricably for the moment in his thoughts, and appealing to his senses, thrilled his impressionable being. He raised his eyes to hers. Should he ever know such happiness again? He released his foot from the stirrup where he had placed it; he hesitated. A glow of joy overspread her face. She stretched out her beautiful arms.

"Oh, come to me," she whispered; "come! come!"

But his eyes fell, the moment of vacillation was past. He could not retreat now, nor would he; he must go forward! He vaulted into the saddle.

"I cannot go back, Sibyl," he said; "I cannot go back now, if I would."

A motion of the rein, a slight pressure of the foot, and the black wheeled. His master did not turn his head, he did not wave his hand. The sure-footed animal clattered down the stony hillside, and he and his rider were lost in the night.

Emanuel had remained at the ford, and there he watched. He emerged from his tree-trunk as Don Enrique came galloping down the path. He laid his hand on the horse's bridle, and shrieked close to the bridegroom's ear, "They from La Primavera have crossed over." He

could scarce make his voice heard above the
noisy flood. "They waited here a little, and
then they crossed. They await the Don Enrique upon the further bank. They told me to
say —" But de Silva waited not to hear; he
paused but for a moment at the river's brink.

"It has indeed risen," he muttered. He
thrust his head forward and peered across the
stream. Over there on the opposite bank the
mompoia leaves waving in the night breeze
seemed to beckon him on. He called. It
seemed to him that answering voices echoed
from the direction of the sand cove. The water
was tossing and foaming in mid-stream, but if
they had just crossed over, might he not also
pass? He struck spurs to his horse, and dashed
out on the line of the ford.

They found him down in the delta where the
waters separate and run out to the sea; his body
bruised and blackened by the jagged rocks upon
which it had been tossed in its long whirling
passage through the rapids; those seething
wreaths of foam, hiding sharp points of rock
which no human thing could meet and live.
He was lying in an eddying pool, close under
the bank, where his sleeve had caught upon a
thorny behucca. His ankle was broken from
the wrench which it had received when the

horse was overthrown by the entangling wire; and when his clothing was removed they found the mark of a hoof upon his fine skin. In that same pool were floating some orange blossoms; for Roberto's fate had been the same.

A fair girl with sad eyes wept over the form, beautiful as a young god, which Sibyl, her eyes dry, her burning lips set in a faint smile, had prepared for burial. Sibyl's were the hands which found and took from the well-known shelf the dainty silken night-robe to be used for the last time; Sibyl's the hands which spread the linen afresh on couch and pillow; Sibyl's the tender hands that drew the sheet up over the calm face; Sibyl's the hand that closed the shutter; Sibyl's the eyes that, staring wide, watched by his couch the long night through.

There was no one to suggest or to object. She laid him just at the edge of Paul's orange grove; the fresh mound overshadowed by glossy branches, stripped bare of blossoms.

THE CHOIR INVISIBLE.

By JAMES LANE ALLEN,

Author of "A Summer in Arcady," "A Kentucky Cardinal," etc.

12mo.   Cloth. $1.50.

"'The Choir Invisible' bears upon its front that unspeakable repose, that unhurried haste which is the hall-mark of literature; it is alive with the passion of beauty and of pain; it vibrates with that incommunicable thrill which Stevenson called the tuning-fork of art. It is distinguished by a sweet and noble seriousness, through which there strains the sunny light of a glancing humour, a wayward fancy, like sunbeams stealing into a cathedral close through stained-glass windows." — *The Bookman.*

"What impresses one most in this exquisite romance of Kentucky's green wilderness is the author's marvellous power of drawing word-pictures that stand before the mind's eye in all the vividness of actuality. Mr. Allen's descriptions of nature are genuine poetry of form and color." — *The Tribune*, New York.

"The impressions left by the book are lasting ones in every sense of the word, and they are helpful as well. Strong, clear-cut, positive in its treatment, the story will become a power in its way, and the novelist-historian of Kentucky, its cleverest author, will achieve a triumph second to no literary man's in the country." — *Commercial Tribune*, Cincinnati.

"It is this mighty movement of the Anglo-Saxon race in America, this first appearance west of the mountains of civilized white types, that Mr. Allen has chosen as the motive of his historical novel. And in thus recalling 'the immortal dead' he has aptly taken the title from George Eliot's greatest poem. It is by far his most ambitious work in scope, in length, and in character drawing, and in construction. And, while it deals broadly with the beginning of the nation, it gains picturesqueness from the author's *milieu*, as hardly anywhere else were the aristocratic elements of colonial life so contrasted with the rugged life of the backwoods." — *The Journal.*

THE MACMILLAN COMPANY.

66 Fifth Avenue, New York.

Works by F. Marion Crawford.

CORLEONE. By F. MARION CRAWFORD, author of "Saracinesca," "Katharine Lauderdale," "Taquisara," etc. Two volumes in box. $2.00.

"Beginning in Rome, thence shifting to Sicily, and so back and forth, the mere local color of the scene of action is of a depth and variety to excite an ordinary writer to extravagance of diction, to enthusiasm, at least of description; the plot is highly dramatic, not to say sensational. . . .

"Our author has created one of the strongest situations wherewith we are acquainted, either in the novel or the drama.

"Then he has rendered an important service to social science, in addition to creating one of the strongest and most delightful novels of our century."
—*The Bookman.*

A ROSE OF YESTERDAY. Cloth. $1.25.

TAQUISARA. Two volumes. 16mo. In box. $2.00.

CASA BRACCIO. With thirteen full-page illustrations from drawings by CASTAIGNE. Buckram. Two volumes in box. $2.00.

ADAM JOHNSTONE'S SON. With twenty-four full-page illustrations by A. FORESTIER. 12mo. Cloth. $1.50.

THE RALSTONS. Two volumes. 16mo. Cloth. $2.00.

Uniform Edition of Mr. Crawford's Other Novels.

12mo. Cloth. Price $1.00 each.

Katharine Lauderdale.
Marion Darche.
A Roman Singer.
An American Politician.
Paul Patoff.
Marzio's Crucifix.
Saracinesca.
A Tale of a Lonely Parish.
Zoroaster.
Dr. Claudius.
Mr. Isaacs.
Children of the King.

Pietro Ghisleri.
Don Orsino. A Sequel to "Saracinesca," and "Sant' Ilario."
The Three Fates.
The Witch of Prague.
Khaled.
A Cigarette-Maker's Romance.
Sant' Ilario. A sequel to "Saracinesca."
Greifenstein.
With the Immortals.
To Leeward.

THE MACMILLAN COMPANY,
66 Fifth Avenue, New York.

ALFRED LORD TENNYSON.

A MEMOIR.

BY

HIS SON.

8vo.   Cloth.   Two Vols.   Price, $10.00, *net.*

These volumes of over 500 pages each contain many letters written or received by Lord Tennyson, to which no other biographer could have had access, and in addition a large number of poems hitherto unpublished.

Several chapters are contributed by such of his friends as Dr. Jowett, the Duke of Argyll, the late Earl of Selborne, Mr. Lecky, Professor Francis T. Palgrave, Professor Tyndall, Mr. Aubrey de Vere, and others, who thus express their personal recollections.

There are many illustrations, engraved after pictures by Richard Doyle, Samuel Lawrence, G. F. Watts, R.A., etc., in all about twenty full-page portraits and other illustrations.

COMMENTS.

"The biography is easily the biography not only of the year, but of the decade, and the story of the development of Tennyson's intellect and of his growth — whatever may be the varying opinions of his exact rank among the greatest poets — into one of the few masters of English verse, will be found full of thrilling interest, not only by the critic and student of literature, but by the average reader."
— *The New York Times.*

"Two salient points strike the reader of this memoir. One is that it is uniformly fascinating, so rich in anecdote and marginalia as to hold the attention with the power of a novel. In the next place, it has been put together with consummate tact, if not with academic art. . . .

"It is authoritative if ever a memoir was. But, we repeat, it has suffered no harm from having been composed out of family love and devotion. It is faultless in its dignity." — *The New York Tribune.*

THE MACMILLAN COMPANY,

66 Fifth Avenue, New York.

THE LETTERS OF ELIZABETH BARRETT BROWNING.

EDITED WITH BIOGRAPHICAL ADDITIONS

BY

FREDERICK G. KENYON.

With portraits. In two volumes. Crown 8vo. $4.00.

Two medium octavo volumes, with portraits, etc. The earliest correspondence quoted took place when the writer was a young girl, and every period of her life is represented in these frank and simple letters. She knew many interesting people, was in Paris during the *coup d'état* in 1851, and lived in Florence during years of great excitement in Italy. Among other pen-pictures she gives one of the few English sketches we have of George Sand, whom she met several times.

"The letters of Elizabeth Barrett Browning are an interesting contribution to the literature of literary correspondence and an agreeable addition to the literature of literary biography."
— *New York Mail and Express.*

"The Browning letters are admirably edited by Mr. Frederick C. Kenyon, who holds them together with biographical notes which give the book an additional value." — *Philadelphia Press.*

"Not since the publication of 'The Letters of Agassiz' has there been a nobler revelation of character in a biographical volume."
— *Boston Evening Transcript.*

"The letters now presented to the public are precisely as they came from the pen of the writer, and we are reminded that it is Mrs. Browning's character, and not her genius, which is delineated in these valuable contributions to literature. . . ."
— *New York Commercial Advertiser.*

THE MACMILLAN COMPANY,
66 Fifth Avenue, New York.